THE HAUNTING

OF

HELLFLEET POINT

LIGHTHOUSE

CAT KNIGHT

Disclaimer

This story is a work of fiction any resemblance to people is purely coincidence. All places, names, events, businesses, etc. are used in a fictional manner. All characters are from the imagination of the author.

Table of Contents

Prologue..1

Chapter One – Driven Out 7

Chapter Two – The Ghosts of Hellfleet 13

Chapter Three – The Shock of Erma........................21

Chapter Four – A Dangerous Slip 27

Chapter Five – Unfathomable Noises......................33

Chapter Six- The Legacy...39

Chapter Seven- Screams on the Wind.....................45

Chapter Eight- The Message 51

Chapter Nine- Nora's Decision...............................55

Chapter Ten- The Search for the Secret 61

Chapter Eleven- Paranormal Demands 71

Chapter Twelve- The Reluctant Ghost 79

Chapter Thirteen- Attack of the Ravens..................83

Chapter Fourteen- Floyd's Gift 93

Here is Your Preview of The Haunting of Knoll House 98

Prologue 99

Chapter One - The Withered Town 107

Here is Your Preview of The Haunting of Stone Street Cemetery 112

Chapter One - The Cemetery 113

Chapter Two - The Consequence..................... 125

Other Titles by Cat Knight 130

About the Author..131

RECEIVE THE HAUNTING OF LILAC HOUSE FREE!...........132

Prologue

Hellfleet Point Lighthouse
Bristol
United Kingdom
8th May 2016

For Floyd Taylor, the 8th of May was the most important day of the year. More important than Christmas or Easter Monday or New Year Eve. It was, the most significant day in Floyd's life. Because that was the day that people stopped shooting at him. It was VE day. A day hardly remembered in contemporary England or anywhere else for that matter. As the years rolled by there were fewer and fewer memories of that day.

Victory in Europe Day was the day that Floyd unpacked his old army tunic, his thirty-seven pattern trousers, and his moth-chewed wool beret. His original boots and puttees had been put in the rubbish decades earlier, but he was certain no one would demote him for not wearing regulation footgear—if it were ever possible that he could be demoted. As he remembered things, he was pretty much the low man on the totem pole.

On VE Day, Floyd, straightened his ninety-year-old spine, puffed out his chest and fought to control his shaking hands as he slipped on the beret.

When he was finished, he studied himself in the mirror. Something was missing. His insignia was in place, so what could it be. His brain, as old as his spine, didn't seem to function as well as it used to. Then, he smiled.

Floyd went to the bureau of his bedroom and opened the top drawer. There, he found the worn case he was looking for. His shaking hands managed to remove the Victoria Cross. He stared at the cross a moment before he polished it on his tunic. He attempted to fasten it to the old cloth, and when he pricked his finger, he stopped, somehow assured that a pinprick meant he had seated the medal properly. With a last look in the mirror, Floyd marched out of the bedroom. If his gait didn't match the cadence in his memory, he didn't notice. Perhaps it was better to live in the past if only for one day.

As Floyd passed the kitchen table, he wondered who the tea was for. Then, he remembered it was his tea, so he tasted it. Cold, which fit the memory in his head. He couldn't count the times he had been served cold tea during the war — more times than hot he thought. A blast of pungent odour hit Floyd, and he shuddered.

"No," Floyd said out loud. "Not today." He shook his fist at nothing in particular. "You will NOT pull your shenanigans today!"

He looked around the room, and everything appeared to be in place. Putting down the tea, he marched through the door that led to the breezeway that led to the tower. It was exactly fifty small steps from the cottage to the tower stairs. He looked up the stairs, took a deep breath, and started.

Halfway up the stairs, Floyd took a rest, a "fiver" as the old sergeant used to call it. He glanced at his feet and discovered he hadn't changed out of his ratty slippers, and his ratty slippers were slick from sliding his feet along the floor.

But he wasn't about to descend just to change shoes. He would simply be a bit more careful. He took a deep breath. Annoyance sent a fleeting pucker over his face, as the familiar odour wafted around him and filled his nostrils. The odour that had plagued him since he bought the place.

"Didn't I tell you?" Floyd said. "NOT TODAY!" He'd fought and won against better enemies than this. Floyd had a strong mind and a stronger will. It kept him going all these years, even in the war. "You'll get your comeuppance one day. You mark my words." He shook his fist into the air.

Floyd didn't know if he took a 'fiver' or a 'tenner', but when he felt stronger, he proceeded up the steps. As with the year before, Floyd asked himself why he had ever purchased Hellfleet.

The lighthouse was no longer functional, but both cottage and tower were sound, and it provided a fantastic view when he bothered to climb the steps which wasn't often. Views were for young people, weren't they? Old men like Floyd always seemed to look down, not out. And if Hellfleet had its peculiarities, well, that went with the territory.

Floyd scooted around the old light and opened the door to the narrow platform and looked out onto its wire mesh and metal railing.

Battered by time it creaked in places, and Floyd wasn't certain about the steadiness of it, or his own steadiness for that matter. But the warm sunshine made him smile and he stepped carefully on to it.

Ravens circled overhead, as if he was going to feed them or something. He never did.

They were nuisance enough the way they were, always cawing at him every-time he stepped outside the door. Grabbing the railing, Floyd looked down on the waves crashing into the rocks far below. The view was spectacular but looking down caused his head to swim a little, and he grabbed the railing tighter and edged away. He wasn't the young man he once was and he wasn't up here for the view. It was VE Day, Floyd had a duty. Pulling himself as erect as he could, Floyd saluted the direction he believed represented London, and began to sing GOD SAVE THE QUEEN in a quavering voice barely above a whisper.

Before he could finish, that damned smell blew around him on the wind.

"Can't you leave me in peace for just this one day?" Floyd called into the developing gust. His jacket flapped about him as he gripped the railing for just a moment to steady himself. The poorly fastened Victoria Cross fell off Floyd's tunic and rolled onto the mesh grate a few feet away. Frowning, and cursing, Floyd stopped singing and moved two steps to retrieve the medal.

That was when the raven swooped.

Floyd knew that ravens liked shiny things, but he never guessed a raven would go after his cross.

That seemed terribly unfair. But ravens didn't play fair, did they, at least these ones never had, and it this one was cockier than usual, probably because it was huge.

"You bloody big blighter," he muttered at it, trying to hit it away.

The raven snatched up the cross and flapped its wings to rise. Perhaps it would have flown away if not for the wind.

A gust blew the bird right at Floyd, whose reflexes seemed a gilded present from yesteryear. He plucked the bird out of the air. His old Sarge would have been proud,

But not for long.

The bird dropped the medal and flapped for open skies. The lurch was too much for Floyd's tottering legs. Hanging onto the raven as if it might save him, Floyd lurched back toward the railing.

A younger Floyd might have caught himself despite the slick slippers. He would have thought quickly enough to release the bird and grab the railing and he wouldn't have tipped over the railing and plummeted like a stone.

The spring wind gusted again, and the Victoria Cross scudded across the mesh. It fell off the edge where the wind shoved it into a crevice by one of the platforms supports. It lodged there, and despite the wind's best efforts, it stayed.

If the cross could have leaned out a bit, it would have seen what was left of Floyd on the most important day of the year. But that's not what happened and both Floyd and the cross were lost.

If indeed it had been a younger Floyd, then he wouldn't have been discovered smashed on the rocks still clutching a dead raven.

Chapter One – Driven Out

Hellfleet Point Lighthouse
Bristol
United Kingdom
January 2018

Nora Hughes smiled at the camera over her middle screen. She knew that her image was being seen in San Francisco, Singapore, Sydney, Tel Aviv, and Frankfurt. She knew her fellow designers were all on board because she could see their faces in the two screens flanking the one directly in front of her. They were online because NIGHT OF THE DEAD, their latest project was ninety percent finished, but even at ninety percent, it was still a week behind schedule. The company wanted the game to beat their biggest competitor to the market, and she was doing her best to finish it.

But this was a team effort. She couldn't do it all herself. While she was pretty and curvy and young, she couldn't rely on looks to get her team to work. She needed commitment.

"OK, folks," she said, knowing her English was being translated into the languages needed. "We're a week behind, and while I can live with that, I can't live with non-commitment.

And I include me, for the next thirty days, we need head down, bum up. No days off, no weekends off, no sleep if you can arrange it. We're very close to publishing the best damn game since Pong—for those of you who never heard of the game. Let's not slack off now. I guarantee that once the game is launched, you will have all the time you want, until the new offers arrive. When this game goes viral, we'll all be able to write our own ticket. Now, a show of hands. Are you with me?"

On the screens, everyone raised their hands. Nora's smile widened. They were all in, and they knew what she expected.

"Then, I won't keep you. You know your assignments. Get to work. Should any of you run into a problem, get to me immediately. While I don't have a lot of assets in reserve, I have a few. Good luck."

She tapped a key and the two side screens went dark. The middle screen still showed her smiling face, but that disappeared as she typed. Her left screen filled with code, and her right screen filled with graphics. The middle screen brought up her email. She had a status report to produce, and she was certain that her boss would love what she was going to write. All she needed to complete the meeting was a cup of tea.

~~~~~

In the kitchen of the smallish flat, Nora grabbed a teabag and waited for the water to hiss. While she waited, she thought about how her life was progressing.

She and Felix, her significant other, had leased the flat because it was as close as they could get to central London where Felix worked in finance, and she met with the game company managers.

Did she love the arrangement? Hardly. The area was crowded and loud and full of people who came and went on a whim, sometimes in as little as two weeks. And, on any given night, the street below would fill with chanters of one strain or another who would carry on long past when normal people slept. Nora was a night owl who liked working late—if it was quiet. There was no benefit in working when the street din drowned out her thoughts.

The kettle boiled, and Nora moved to fill her cup, just before the incredibly deep thump penetrated the room. For a moment, she didn't move although her eyes turned to the direction of the next-door flat. The bass sound was unusual during the day, usually, heavy metal music always arrived at night. During the day, at least, she didn't have to cope with this level of inconsiderate sound. But if the last couple of weeks were any indication, there was a worse problem than that.

She whirled and sprinted back to her computer room, hoping that the computers would be alright.

She was too late.

The screens were black. Her computers were dead. Her hands curled into fists, and she pounded her chair.

"No, no, no, no, NO!" She said. "I can't work this way!"

As sure as fog comes to London, the loud music had overtaxed the electrical system.

The breakers had tripped, and the power was out. While she was somewhat used to it at night, she couldn't abide the interruption during the day. Worse, she knew who was responsible. His name was Mercury or Copper or something metal, and he couldn't live if he didn't max out his speakers.

She had talked to him ten times, and every time, he acted as if he didn't understand. Slack jawed, tattooed, pierced like a voodoo doll, he always nodded in agreement and went right back to what he was doing. She thought that if she possessed a firearm, she would march up to him and simply end his miserable existence forever.

Knowing that it would take some minutes for the manager to reset the breakers, Nora returned to the kitchen. Luckily, she could still make tea.

~~~~~

"He did it again, and this time during the day," Nora said.

Felix nodded. At the end of a long day of trades, he looked tired. Blonde, blue-eyed, Felix, on a good day, was as handsome as an actor. Nora had met him right after he had lost yet one more audition. In the pub, he looked totally overcome, which appealed to her instincts.

After several long dates, she convinced him that perhaps acting was not his forte. Since he was good with numbers, why didn't he give finance a go? She never knew if it was the adeptness with numbers or her entreaty that got him into the trading game, and she didn't care.

He was a good man, and she believed him when he told her he loved her.

"We have to move," Nora said. "I can't work like this."

Felix smiled and sipped his vodka on the rocks.

"You don't know what it's like," Nora said.

"I thought that it would be all right during the day, but Mercury kicked me offline this afternoon, and you know how long it takes to reboot everything. I can't have it."

"Where do you propose we go? And his name is Pewter."

"How would I know? Felix, I don't ask for much. I don't demand like some women. But I love my job, and I'm damned good at my job, but I can't do my job if the power cuts out every fifteen minutes."

He stood and held his arms open. She went to him, and he hugged her.

"I tell you what," he said. "Tomorrow, I'll start looking for a new flat or house or place where you can work without interruption. I don't expect I'll find something right away, but I promise I will find something. Deal?"

"Deal," she said and kissed him.

Two days later, while she was engrossed in a game-wide test, she received a text from Felix. She glanced at it.

"I've found it," the text read. "Tell you after work."

Smiling, Nora put down the phone and returned to the test game. If this went well... she'd have it done and dusted.

She prayed Mercury wasn't home to trip the breakers.

Chapter Two – The Ghosts of Hellfleet

Felix set the pint in front of Nora and slid into the seat opposite her. His smile reassured her. He seemed almost giddy.

"Before you say no," Felix began. "I want you to picture the sea, waves breaking over rocks. A calm seclusion where the only sounds you hear all day are the calls of the gulls. A place where the power supply never goes out or gets cut or even fades and where the communications are second to none."

"And where is this Shangri-La?" she asked.

He pulled a printout from his pocket and slid it across the table. "Take a look."

She opened the page and stared. "You've got to be kidding."

"Before you say no, the cottage has three bedrooms and two loos. One of the bedrooms can be converted into an office. The train depot in St. George is minutes away, and the ride to London is less than an hour. When I said it has great communication and power capacity, it's because those were essential while it was functional, which it no longer is, but we just need to get an electrician in and make sure it's all up to grade."

"But it's a lighthouse," Nora protested.

"Precisely. Hellfleet is on the ocean and pretty much all by itself. And it's a steal. It came on the market because the old geezer who owned it didn't have heirs. I already put quid against it because it really is prime real-estate. I've arranged to take tomorrow afternoon off so we can do a quick look-see."

Nora opened her mouth to say something. He raised his hand. "Don't ask me why I think highly of a place I've never seen, because I don't know. I just have the feeling that it will meet our needs."

"OK. It's got a helluva name, but apart from that, do you really want to commute every day?"

"For a while. I think that after a bit, they'll let me work from home. After all, I can trade from anywhere."

Nora looked from the image of the lighthouse to Felix, and she could feel his excitement. At first blush, it did look decidedly better than their cramped flat. Ocean, salt air, a place of their own, there weren't many drawbacks.

"And it comes furnished, we barely have to move."

"OK, but what about all the old geezer stuff that's there? You get to remove any of his stuff I don't want and get rid of it."

"Gladly. I'll donate it. Everyone is looking for geezer stuff, aren't they? It's retro."

~~~~~

The next day, Nora used the GPS on her phone to guide them. Well, she tried to use it.

14

The coverage that far from London reception dipped in and out. After traveling down the wrong road, twice, they decided to find a pub, lunch, and directions.

Over bangers and mash, they asked the waitress how to find Hellfleet Point Lighthouse.

"Where?" the waitress asked, her eyebrows shooting up to her hairline and voice edging toward incredulous.

"The lighthouse," Felix said. "Hellfleet."

"I'm not at all sure you want to go there," the waitress said warningly.

"Why, it was only a few weeks ago that the daft old codger jumped off the platform and smashed hissself on the rocks."

"I believe he slipped," Felix said.

"More likely, the ghost shoved him. There's a ghost there you know. Old Woody don't much like anyone at the Fleet."

Nora gazed down into her tea while Felix cleared his throat awkwardly.

"Oh, is that so? Well, how intriguing. Well, we're here now… and since we are… we'd just like to have a look at the old place."

The waitress gave them another 'you've been warned' look before drawing a rough map on a serviette.

~~~~~

"You didn't mention anything about a ghost," Nora said as Felix drove down a narrow lane.

"Because neither of us believes in ghosts."

"Full disclosure, Felix, full disclosure. What about the ghost?"

Felix shrugged, "I don't know all the fine print, but it seems some locals believe a spirit haunts the lighthouse. But the lighthouse dates from the seventeenth century. Anything that old is always haunted."

Nora wanted to pursue the ghost aspect, but at that moment they rolled over a dune and caught their first glance of Hellfleet. White, tall, it stood stark against the dull grey of the ocean.

"Besides," Felix said. "Ghost or not, you're going to love this place."

And Nora did fall in love with Hellfleet. It's rough and rocky shore and washed stone cottage seemed like it held a secret, a little bit of magic. Nora believed in magic, as much as she believed in ghosts but its charm wormed its way into her psyche and she wanted it.

Every window held a view. And the rooms were light and airy. The bedroom she decided would be theirs, was the one that adjoined a small courtyard with a bench that looked out to rocky crags, where the ocean beat against the rocks. She thought she might even put in a sliding door, so that they might enjoy direct access to it.

The room she had chosen to be converted into her office, was positioned was such that it bordered the rocks and looked out directly to the ocean. With its small square windows, it offered a nice view that would allow her some space to think, yet not enough to distract her if she didn't want it to. *The bed would have to go though.*

Contemplating the space, something caught Nora's eye. It stuck out from under the legs of the bed.

Bending down Nora found an old trunk which, after she had pulled it out, snapped open easily. A strong smell of moth balls caused her to close her hand around her nose. Immediately she could see that it contained an old man's clothing.

Rifling through she found no more than this, and a single pair of worn, brown boots.

"Old geezer stuff here," she called out to Felix. He didn't answer, but she knew he would get rid of it.

They meandered around the cottage and made their way to the winding stairs in the tower that led to the lantern room and the platform. Nora stood on the metal mesh and looked outward, watching the gulls soar.

The breeze ruffled her hair, and Felix embraced her. She snuggled in. Hellfleet was more romance novel than real life.

"Like it?" he asked.

"You knew I would."

"I'm told it can be a rough go when the winter storms hit."

"I don't care. I'll be safe and warm and turning out the most fantastic games ever. I can think right now of a dozen ways to use this. It reminds me of something from a Tolkien book."

"Don't say Mordor," Felix warned. "We do not want to curse this place."

"There are no curses," Nora said. "And this is painted white, not black. It's more Gondor than Mordor."

"Whatever you say, game maker. I'll bow to your superior knowledge of fantasy and magic kingdoms with monsters around every corner."

"If you're going to build a sword-and-sorcery land, you have to do your research."

"Just leave the demons and dragons out of our house, OK?"

"They'll exist solely in the nether world of games. For us, it's sunshine and smooth sailing."

They walked from the lookout and along the platform, back down the winding stairs. On the wind, a musical lilt almost caught Nora's attention, if the buffeting of the old structures hadn't been so loud perhaps she would have heard clearly the man's voice, faint, weak, and rasping out GOD SAVE THE QUEEN—

~~~~~

Nora weaved the move into her tight schedule, but she did find time to tell Mercury-Pewter that he could take his testosterone-driven speakers and put them where the sun don't shine. She knew such talk was definitely not ladylike, but she didn't care. The confrontation was too satisfying.

Once In the cottage, her first priority was setting up her office. Deadlines didn't disappear because she was moving. The packed boxes would have to wait until after she had held a status meeting with her team. Everything would have to wait for that milestone, and that milestone was reached long after Felix had gone to bed.

Although elated, Nora didn't wake him. She slipped into bed and looked out the window at the moon. That was the last thing she remembered before the morning sun filtered through, and she woke to find herself alone. Felix had left on his commute.

With contented sigh, she snuggled back under the covers. A few more moments of blissful daydreaming and then the sound of the kettle hissing got her attention.

Perhaps Felix hadn't left yet? He should have but... She slipped into a robe and started for the kitchen. When she got there, she stopped cold.

"Who are you?" Nora asked.

Chapter Three – The Shock of Erma

An old woman fussed at the counter with a teapot. She turned but didn't smile.

"I'm Erma," the woman said. "I clean this place."

Annoyance surged over Nora. "And you got in... how?"

"Oh, I have a key," Erma said. "Floyd gave it to me because he couldn't remember when I was coming. He got a bit addled at the end. Half the time, he thought he was still in the war. Called me nurse when he was that way. At first, I tried to correct him, but that didn't do nothing. So, I became the 'nurse'. Didn't change anything. I did my job, and if he had wanted me in a nurse's getup, well, I would have drawn a line there. Cleaning is fine, daydreams are something else again." Erma poured boiling water into the tea kettle. "How do you take your tea?"

"I'm sorry, but I wasn't aware Floyd had a cleaner. You're a bit of a surprise."

"I understand. The cleaner ain't included in the will, is she now? So, how do you like your rugs? I can vacuum every day if you wish."

Nora walked past her, pulled a cup from the cupboard and faced Erma.

"I'm not certain I need a cleaner."

"I don't do windows, dearie. You can never get windows right, so I don't even try. But I do know a bloke who will make them like crystal, and he don't cost an arm and a leg."

Nora frowned as Erma stood, shuffled over, and grabbed the cup out of Nora's hand. Nora gaped as Erma made a cup of tea.

"I do tea because everyone needs tea, and when you're sick I'll bring a bit of chicken soup." Erma winked. "A hot toddy ain't out of the question either."

"We should talk about your employment," Nora said.

"Don't worry your pretty head. What Floyd give me was quite enough — unless you want me to come three days instead of two. Then, we have to chat. I've got other houses on those days."

Erma handed over the cup of tea.

"I do laundry and dishes as long as they're reasonable. Some like to take advantage by letting things pile up, so I'm giving notice right now. But you don't look like that type which does that." Erma touched Nora's arm. "And I want to assure you that I don't do wine or spirits while I'm workin'. Some cleaners do, but not Erma. No, ma'am."

Erma turned and started away. "Time to get to work." She paused and turned back to Nora. "Last, I don't work at night. I'm gone a good hour before sundown if you please."

With a nod, Erma turned and left the room.

For a minute, Nora wasn't exactly sure what had happened. When she woke this morning, it was just her and Felix. Now, she had 'Erma', and she came with a seemingly long list of stipulations. How had that happened? She knew she should chase the woman down and set things right, but that prospect didn't appeal - she was just an old lady after-all.

Sipping tea, Nora decided that the problem of Erma could wait until Felix came home. After all, Erma would be cleaning for Felix too.

Smiling at her logic, Nora added more tea to her cup and started for her office.

~~~~~

"Well," Felix said as he buttered his bread. "How much will this Erma cost?"

"That's just it," Nora replied. "I don't know. "No more than it cost Floyd. She guaranteed that."

"You hired a cleaner without knowing what she costs?"

"More like inherited a cleaner. And I'm sure it can't be too much. A pensioner like Floyd couldn't afford much, could he?"

Felix quizzed her. "It's not like you to tolerate someone in your space. She shrugged.

"This place is bigger than the flat. I could probably use the extra time it would give me."

"She sounds doddery and old, you'll probably have to wash the dishes again after she's gone."

"I'd be a terrible person to get rid of her for nothing. She seems to have been around forever. And she's not exactly doddery, on the way maybe but not there yet."

Felix scoffed then laughed.

"If your crew could see you now. What's that name they call you? Cruella? I say they've got you all wrong."

Nora tried to look hurt, but she really didn't care. She had heard it said about her a couple of times, just because she wanted to get the projects off the ground and flying in on time. Her competitiveness is what kept her at the top of her game. She worked hard and her crew had to as well.

"Oh, come on... I'm not that bad!"

"You remind me of a burned marshmallow. Hard and crusty on the outside, but soft and melty in the middle."

He laughed again and bit into the bread. Half wanting to argue about it, she stopped and laughed with him instead, there was a grain of truth in every criticism after-all. They were still smiling when the cold draft blew over them.

"Window open?" Felix asked.

"I don't think so," she answered.

"I'll look."

She hugged herself as Felix left the table. Would Erma have left a window open? Erma didn't wash windows, so it didn't seem likely. Yet, perhaps if she had opened it she'd just done it to air the place out.

"Back bedroom," Felix said as he re-entered the kitchen. "Must've been the new maid"

"She's not a maid. She's a cleaner, and she doesn't do windows. So, I'm wondering why she opened it."

"Just ask her. I'm sure she'll have a perfectly fine explanation."

~~~~~

Nora worked solidly for several hours, long after Felix had gone to bed. While she felt like sleeping, she knew she had work to complete and tired as she was, her thoughts kept running around in circles. She tapped a key and pushed the problem of Erma from her mind. Nora hadn't yet decided if she was going to keep the cleaner or let her go. That decision could wait.

For just a moment, she wondered about the open window, and made a mental note to ask Erma the next time the cleaner appeared. Nora didn't want Erma leaving behind open windows. That wouldn't do. Years of city living had taught her caution.

As the screens came alive, colour flooded her eyes. She forgot about Erma and the window. The opening screen shots of NIGHT OF THE DEAD appeared, and she had to admit the graphics were awesome.

CAT KNIGHT

Chapter Four – A Dangerous Slip

The smell wasn't the smell of a rotting carcass or eggs gone bad. It was a pungent body odour akin to how a fisherman might smell, a fishy, dirty human body. The smell stung her nose and made her look up from her screen.

"Felix are you out there? Has something gone off in the fridge?"

No answer was forthcoming. She got up and left the office. There were no lights on, and Felix was not in the kitchen. *Maybe when he checked that window earlier, he had checked others and accidentally unlatched one.* Nora knew that didn't make sense, but she wanted an explanation. Yellow light flooded the rooms as she switched them on, checking rooms. The odour wafted around her not seeming to be stronger in any one place than another.

The light house, so far away from any other homes, had no curtains and a sense of vulnerability niggled at her.

She was keenly aware that the night was pitch black, anyone looking in could see her, and she would have no idea they were there.

As she walked into the spare room she quickly shut the lights off and tiptoed toward the window. She could see nothing but the night sky, scattered with stars and moonlight streaming in through the glass panes. *But if someone was close enough to bring that smell with them, they wouldn't be outside anyway....* She made quickly for the light.

As she stepped, her foot skidded and Nora's feet went out from under her. A searing pain tore through her forehead and everything before her eyes swam. She heard Felix call to her and was vaguely aware of him laying her down on the bed.

Felix put a cold cloth to her temple. His face was drawn and worry etched his eyes.

"What happened?" she mumbled.

"You slipped I guess. On part of a fish by the look of it. A damned seagull or a raven must have brought it in through that open window. I must've missed it when I was in here before. They're always bloody well hopping around it seems. Blasted things. I didn't think they'd have the gumption for that though. Maybe the old fellow fed them or something."

He continued wiping her forehead.

"You've got a cut on your head. What were you doing walking around in the dark anyway?"

"Did I black out?"

"No, I don't think so, if you did it was only a second or two."

"There was a smell in the office. I couldn't think where it came from, it was so strong."

She laughed a bit to ease the tension.

28

"I guess I'm working too hard I thought there might be someone in here... or maybe lurking outside... I turned off the light to look outside properly and then I went to turn it back on and I slipped."

Felix's look said everything she knew he was thinking. *You thought there was someone in here because of a smell?* She rubbed his arm.

"I don't know... I'm just tired, my imagination is probably getting caught up in the sinister world of 'Night of the Dead'. Anyway, it just seemed to be so... near to me."

"I'll check around and make sure we're alone and locked up. But let's get you to bed now." Felix helped Nora up. As her feet touched the floor her foot kicked something.

"What's that boot doing there?" Annoyance punctuated every word and she brushed her hand over the welt on her forehead.

"It was in the trunk, I know it was." Tiredness overwhelmed her, all Nora wanted was sleep. "Oh, I don't know! Maybe Erma took it on herself to clean some of this stuff out."

Felix bent down to retrieve it, a slight frown crossed his brow. "Looks like you were in luck." His fingers fiddled with a large nail that had sprung up from its old wooden floor. The laces in the boot wound around it. "You missed out on a really nasty injury. I'll have to do a check for others."

~~~~~

When Nora entered the kitchen the next morning, she half expected to find Erma at the table.

29

But Erma wasn't there, which reminded Nora that Erma cleaned twice a week. Felix, had left early, she practically had to force him to go.

"I'll be fine, you've got a meeting."

"Are you sure, you're ok. I can take a day..."

"No. Go. Go." She got out of bed and almost pushed him out the door before climbing back in for another forty winks.

As she ate breakfast and sipped tea, rain beat on the windows. Despite the oddly found fish and the fall, she had slept well and now she formulated what would happen next in her game.

For the successful player, the next level would pop up. For the loser, back to start. The game was cruel—just like real life. The sound of a car crunching on gravel drew her eyes to the window. A taxi cab pulled into the drive.

~~~~~

"What are you doing home?" she asked.

"Why? Got a lover stashed away some place?"

"Why would you think that?"

He rushed over and kissed her cheek.

"I don't. Come with me. I have to pack."

She followed him to the bedroom and watched as he snatched a suitcase from the closet and started pulling clothes from the bureau.

30

"I'm not there five minutes before Virgil calls me into his office. He asks if I'm ready for a trip, which is like asking if I'm ready for a promotion. I say absolutely, and he sends me home to pack."

"Great," Nora said. "But where are you going?"

He beamed at her.

"New York. We're going to New York to hobnob with some big names in the biz."

"I don't get it, why?"

"Don't you see? They're thinking about opening an office in New York, and they want to make sure I can get along with the Yanks."

"We're moving to New York?"

"No, yes, maybe." He grabbed suits from the closet. "I'm sure it's just an overture, a feeling things out sort of a thing. But they picked me, me!" He packed with more speed than she thought possible.

"How long will you be gone?" she asked.

"Three, four days, no longer."

He stopped, looked at her, and came over.

"I'm getting ahead of everything, aren't I?" He hugged her. "I should have asked if you were all right with this."

"Of course, I'm all right," she said. "It's a great career move, isn't it?"

"You're my great career move," he answered. "I'd still be making parody videos if I hadn't met you. Are you sure?"

"Well we did just move…" Nora said, backtracking on her thoughts.

"I don't think the decision has been made, and once it is, it will take months to set up an office. So, you'll, have time to learn to speak Yank."

She laughed. "You're insane, and I love you for it."

He released her and finished his packing. She watched, both happy and wondering. Things were moving far too fast.

He closed the suitcase, looked around the room, and grabbed her for a kiss.

"You'll call when you get there?" she asked.

"Email, text, and voice. I'll soon be a nuisance. Careful on the floor boards. If you find any more nails, put some electrical tape around it, until I can check the boards properly."

She watched till the taxi that had brought him from St. George disappeared in the distance. For a moment, she was sad. A week without Felix was… a week without Felix.

A week without Felix wasn't ideal, but alone, she could move the game right along. Closing and locking the door behind her, she grabbed the cast iron frying pan and banged the offending nail back in. She marched back to the kitchen for the next cup of tea that would power her for the following few hours.

Nora was an hour into a productive session when the sound rolled into the room.

Chapter Five –
Unfathomable Noises

It was one of those sounds that seemed to come from everywhere and nowhere.

A mixture of annoyance, tiredness and frustration rushed out from Nora in a loud sigh. She left her office and went into the main room. The scraping hadn't become louder or softer. It just kept continuing on at the same level, which irked her that she couldn't locate it. She walked around the room, listening carefully. Did it come from outside? That made no sense unless there was someone else in the lighthouse...

Oh God Nora, not this again. Pull yourself together. But she couldn't. Every hair began to stand on end. Furious with herself she inwardly yelled. *GET. A. GRIP.* She remembered that she had definitely locked the door behind her.

Just to be sure, she walked over and tested it. It opened easily.

Now, feeling the calmness that she had forced upon herself leaving her, she wiped sweat from her upper lip. *I know I locked that door. How can it be unlocked? Maybe I didn't?* She couldn't be certain now. Perhaps she remembered another day when she had locked the door.

She couldn't be absolutely sure about anything. So, maybe…

But now, it was unlocked, and Felix was gone. *ERMA! Had Erma come after all?*

"ERMA?" Nora called.

No answer.

Nora consciously locked the door and tried it.

She could call the police but that would make her sound like a paranoid idiot. *Would you please come out and check my house just in case, that maybe, possibly, someone sneaked in while I wasn't looking? No, that sounded like some hysterical woman, scared of her own shadow.* And that wasn't Nora. At least not usually. But the door was unlocked and there was the scraping, and she needed to make certain she was alone.

Making her way to the knives she picked up the sharpest of them, but within a second reconsidered, and gently tucked it, and the rest of them, under the tea towels. If some-one was here, a stronger someone with bad intent, that knife could be easily taken away from her.

What could she use then?

Instead of a knife, she went to the kitchen and grabbed a ceramic mug. If she threw it, she might distract him, allowing her to get away. She had to admit the mug wasn't the best weapon in the world, but it would have to do. Gripping it tightly, she began her search.

The main room and the kitchen were easy. No trespassers but no end to the scraping either. As she moved into the bedrooms, she tried to pinpoint it. But it didn't seem to be anywhere in particular.

The only thing she was sure of, was that the scraping was somewhere and it wasn't letting up. Nora walked quietly to the master bedroom. It was vacant, and since she had just left her office, she was sure that this room was vacant too. As she eased into the spare bedroom she glanced quickly from side to side. No, no one waited for her. Cautiously, she glanced under the bed. At least, the trunk hadn't moved. Feeling a bit better, but frowning, she returned to the kitchen. The scraping hadn't stopped.

That left... the tower.

In for a shilling, in for a quid, she told herself. Holding onto the mug, she passed out the door, through the breezeway, and into the tower. Was the scraping sound louder? She couldn't be sure. She looked around to make sure she was alone. Then, she locked the door so no one could follow her up the stairs and started to climb. Even though she was young, the climb winded her.

At the top of the lighthouse, Nora stopped to look around. Out at sea, a fishing trawler rolled over the waves, she wondered if they saw her too. Somehow it gave her a sense of security.

SCRAPE. SCRAPE. SCRAPE. She knew she had to go out on the platform.

She grasped onto the railing as she inched along, hair flying around her face the wind buffeting against her. She shouldn't have been surprised at the strength of the wind, because the tower was high. Still, it felt like a gale. Despite what the engineer had said about structural integrity, she didn't trust the platform.

Slowly, slowly she moved against the force of the wind around the arc of the circle, and then she saw it.

Nora's mouth dropped open.

The mug slipped from her hand, bounced across the mesh and over the edge. She didn't watch it, and she didn't hear it land, but she knew it had smashed on the rocks. She gripped the railing with both hands.

Brown and worn, the boot from the trunk was tied to the railing. In mesmerised confusion, she decided that it couldn't be the source of the scraping sound. Gripping the railing tighter, she didn't know what to do. The wind whipped her hair, but she didn't let go with even one hand to push it away. Her throat had grown dry with the breeze, and was now constricting from her tension.

As she stared at it, she realized the scraping had stopped. How? Why? She didn't have an answer. After a moment, her throat relaxed and by the grace of God, the wind died down. Nora felt calmer. She wanted to know what the boot meant, but she didn't have a clue. Nora stepped forward and untied the boot with shaking hands.

It was a message, wasn't it? The old, worn, brown boot was supposed to tell her something. Otherwise why was it there. Was it trying to tell her something last night too and she just hadn't seen it? Was that horrible fishy smell supposed to be a message too? If one was, the other was.

Increasingly, as moments passed, Nora convinced herself that they were messages. The ghost was real. Either that, or someone was messing with her. Opting to keep her mind open, at least for now, Nora turned and walked.

With deliberate, calm steps, she made her way back around the platform, over the breezeway, down the steps, unlocking the door and made her way into the cottage.

Replacing the boot in the trunk, she tried to think logically. *Who had a key to Hellfleet?* Felix, herself, Erma for sure, but who else? How many keys might be floating around? For the first time, Nora asked herself what she knew about Hellfleet.

Her knowledge stretched all the way back to... Floyd. And the lighthouse was far older than that, wasn't it? Was there something in the history that she needed to know?

Making sure the trunk was in its place and the doors were locked, she went to her office and faced the screens. The game would have to wait for an hour or two. She needed to know more about Hellfleet.

~~~~~

Three hours later, Nora peeled herself out of her chair and stretched. Despite all the promises that the Internet held every bit of information available, she had found precious little about Hellfleet. Many sites contained the physical data. Thirty meters high, built long before the invention of electricity, converted several times, and eventually mothballed. She found those facts over and over.

She found two sites that spoke to hauntings. It seemed that on certain moonless nights, people passing by could spot a lone figure atop the tower, staring out to sea. That was supposed to be Clareth Wright who with her husband Daniel tended the lighthouse for over a decade.

37

According to the lore, Daniel went fishing one day and didn't come back. Months later, out of desperation or madness, Clareth jumped to her death.

The figure on the platform was Clareth searching the sea for her missing husband. While Nora thought the story quaint, she didn't believe it. She hadn't seen any apparitions — just scraping and a noxious smell, and that boot.

Remembering that Felix was somewhere over the Atlantic, Nora decided not to cook. St. George was a short drive away, and as she recalled, it had its share of pubs. A night out might be just what she needed.

"If I find a boot out of the trunk when I get back, it's the joining the mug at the bottom of the tower. GOT IT?" she yelled into the cottage, as she locked the door.

Chapter Six - The Legacy

"You're the new light-tender, aren't ya?"

Nora looked up from her phone. The man smiling at her was perhaps fifty. His nose red, his mostly grey beard scruffy, his smile missing a few teeth, he was a pub regular, a man found in every pub in every city and village. A cap covered long, greasy hair. A worn jacket covered worn clothes.

"I'm afraid there's no longer a light to tend," she replied.

"But you're livin' there." He slid onto the chair opposite her. "You bought the devil from that old pensioner."

"Yes, we bought it from Floyd."

"Have you met Woody yet?"

Nora frowned.

"Woody?"

"Elija Ravenwood, Captain Elija Ravenwood."

"I'm afraid not."

The man turned and waved to the barmaid for two more ales. He waited till she nodded before he turned back to Nora.

"If you've not heard of Woody, then you haven't heard of Clareth and Daniel Wright either?"

"I read about them. Rather tragic, don't you think?"

"Aye, but not for them."

"I'm not sure I follow."

"I'm Duncan by the way, but most folks just call me dunce." He laughed at his own joke, and his laugh was cut short by a deep cough. Nora waited, almost certain that she didn't particularly want to continue the conversation.

"Lighten up," Duncan continued. "Without a joke, what do you got?"

"Serenity?" she answered.

He laughed again as the barmaid slid two new ales on the table.

"On the lady," Duncan said.

Nora didn't argue.

Duncan took a pull at the ale before he spoke again. "Elija Ravenwood captained the Wipford, a fair ship with a fair crew. They was comin' back from Cairo with a load of China silk and India tea. November ain't the best month for sailin', and middle of the night ain't the best time to be passin' through the channel, especially with Clareth and Daniel doin' the light."

"I'm sure you mean well—"

"No, missy, no interruptions yet. The story is just beginin'." He shook a dirty finger at her. "Clareth and Daniel moved into Hellfleet, and bad things began to happen. If the stories be right, they sometimes forgot to tend the fire. You know they used a fire in the old days?" Nora nodded, and Duncan seemed to take it as a cue the story was going well.

He leaned in close, his tobacco stained teeth barely away from Nora's face and his tone became conspiratorial.

"Seems they especially forgot when the weather was foul and a well-laden ship was passin'... In the dark of night with the wind and rain slashin' gettin' past Hellfleet ain't guaranteed. They was wreckers you see, makin' sure that ships got wrecked on the rocks, and that point earned its name for the wrecks that happened there." Duncan stopped and nodded his head for effect. "As Capt. Ravenwood found out."

Nora obligingly opened her eyes wide and Duncan continued.

"He floundered out in that black, cold water. His cargo got swept onto the beach. His crew drowned. Ravenwood made it to the beach where Daniel and Clareth were gatherin' cargo. Flotsam and jetsam, if you please. There were a few other scavengers out there that night, and one or two remember Ravenwood's dyin' words."

Duncan stopped, and took a long drink of his ale, Nora sipped hers. She knew the punch line was coming.

"Captain Elija Ravenwood laid Satan's curse on Daniel and his wife. Ravenwood swore revenge on them and all that followed them at the lighthouse. And you know what happened to Clareth and Daniel?"

"Daniel was lost at sea. Clareth jumped to her death," Nora said.

Duncan sat back and laughed softly.

"You've done your homework, I see. But what of the others?"

"Others?"

Duncan winked.

"There were others. Clareth and Daniel were followed by Nathan Smith.

Nathan, if the tales be true, tended the light with a bit more faithfulness, but that didn't keep him from dyin'. Seems the vent for the fire got clogged with a bird or something. He didn't notice the gas. Passed out, and they didn't find him for two days."

Nora's smile faded. She studied Duncan.

"Nathan was followed by the Browns. The Browns was brighter than most. They quit after a month. They couldn't handle the haunting."

"Why are you telling me this?"

"The Browns were followed by Martha and Michael Cogan. The Cogans never even spent one night in Hellfleet. When their cat wouldn't go inside, they thought perhaps the place wasn't for them. Old Charley Mauch lasted two years. Most folks say that was because he spent most of his days seven sheets to the wind. Woody don't seem to bother drunks."

"Who's Woody?"

"You don't get it? Woody is the ghost of Elija Ravenwood. If you haven't met him yet, you soon will."

Nora sipped more ale.

"And after Old Charley?"

"They decommissioned Hellfleet. Stood empty for over fifty years. Takes a while for people to forget."

"How do you know so much?"

"Family's been here since before Clareth and Daniel. Every one of us got warned about Hellfleet."

Duncan finished off his ale and stood.

"I'm guessin' you don't believe in Woody or any ghost, and that's fine. Maybe, he did get tired of hangin' around. I hope, I hope."

Nora watched Duncan weave his way to the bar. She wondered just how much of his story was true. Probably very little. After all, the Internet said absolutely nothing about Elija Ravenwood.

~~~~~

As Nora stepped away from the car, she looked up at the tower platform. Was there a figure looking out to sea? She didn't see any. There was no funny smell when she entered the cottage, and no scraping either.

Just to be sure, she checked the trunk. Both boots were in there. She smiled and headed for her office. With any luck, she would put in some productive time before Felix called.

Felix's call came after Nora had spent two hours at the computer and one hour in bed. She was groggy when she answered the phone, but still Felix's voice was welcome. They didn't talk long.

He was tired, suffering from jet lag. She was half asleep. Good-byes were quick. She settled into her pillow and closed her eyes.

That's when she heard the scream.

Chapter Seven- Screams on the Wind

Nora's eyes popped open. She stared into the dark of the bedroom and felt her heart start to pound. For some seconds, she did absolutely nothing. Her mind couldn't quite determine if she had actually heard a scream, or if her brain had somehow manufactured one. In that nether world between sleep and wakefulness, that layer when dreams seemed clothed in reality, in that place – there was a scream. But was there one for real?

There couldn't be.

Despite her racing heart, logic told her that a scream required a person, and she was quite sure she was all alone. *Except for whoever else might be out there.* She had checked the doors before she went to bed. An unpleasant trickle of fear began in her stomach. She tried to squash it, and lay there, eyes moving left and right, not wanting to move and yet not sure of anything.

The question was whether or not she would be able to go to sleep, or would she lie there all-night waiting for a scream that couldn't come.

"Bloody hell," she said out loud tossing the covers off. Feet into slippers, once more she wondered if she needed a weapon.

At that thought, she stopped. Did she really need to go? Couldn't it be just a dream? Who wouldn't hear a scream after listening to Duncan's stories? She was surprised she didn't see the drowned image of Elija Ravenwood walk through the door.

And then there was the little voice that pleaded with her. *You'll probably be safer hiding right here under the covers.* Still, she couldn't deny her heart. Setting her jaw, she turned on a light and left the room, mobile phone in hand.

Her first search was the kitchen. Nothing. The office. Nothing. The loo, the bathroom, the laundry, the living room, finally, the back bedroom. The place where everything seemed to happen. All turned up nothing.

"Well I'm bloody well not going outside, and absolutely I'm not going up those stairs OR the platform. So, you can just forget it Woody or whoever the hell you are." Her voice sounded braver than she felt.

Feeling foolish for yelling at no-one, Nora marched back into the bedroom. She had found nought. Not a sound, not an odour, not a scream, not a human or a ghost. If "Woody" was hanging around, he was keeping to himself.

Pulling off her slippers and robe she climbed into bed. A frigid draft rushed over the back of her neck and Nora simply dived under the covers still hanging onto her phone. She debated and argued. If she called Felix what could he do? She would just worry him, and she couldn't call the police because she heard a scream and now there was a draft.

No, Nora told herself firmly from under the covers. There couldn't be a draft. The doors and windows were closed.

She just checked them. Yet, she had felt something, and if it was a draft...

She didn't complete the thought. In fact, she didn't want to think at all. Her mind was playing tricks on her.

There had been no scream and no draft, and she wasn't going to act as if there had been.

She made sure the bedroom door was locked. Under the covers she began singing songs in her head, anything to keep her mind off what was going on here. She didn't close her eyes straight away. In fact, she didn't know when she dozed off, but somehow in all of her emotional exhaustion, and remembering Erma would be there in the morning; she slept.

~~~~~

"A question," Nora said as she made a pot of tea. "What do you know about Woody?"

Erma looked at Nora for a few seconds.

"Ah, I see you've met Duncan. You know, for an extra pint, he would have told you all about Bertie and the Tonegal Stone."

"Tonegal?"

"It's a bit of a story, and he loves to tell it — if you buy the ale."

"Then, there's nothing to Clareth and Daniel?"

"I didn't say that, miss. Clareth and Daniel were real and if the stories about them are real, they were as evil as people as you could get. Their habit of letting the fire die sent many a ship onto the shoals."

Nora stirred her tea mindlessly, "And Collingwood?"

"Do you mean Ravenwood? He was real also. The Wipford went down out there in a storm straight from Hell.

Some claim that if the wind is right, you can still hear the sailors screamin'."

"Screaming?"

"I can't vouch for that, I never heard 'em, and I can't say if Ravenwood actually made it to the beach that night. His dyin' curse might be the stuff of unicorn sightings. But it makes for a lively tale to share on a dark night."

"Do you think that Ravenwood, – is real?"

"Woody? As real as your imagination." Erma stopped working and stared into Nora's eyes. "The ravens around this place are real, and they make a mischief once on a while. And on occasion I find a window that shouldn't be open and a draft that comes and goes and maybe a real strong smell of seaweed and rotten fish. But I wouldn't give the credit to Woody. There's gulls as well as ravens out there, and they bring all sorts up onto the rocks. Take a look and you'll see a hundred different kinds of broken shells and the like. Bits of fish too."

"But you always go home before dark," Nora said. "Why?"

Erma returned to her work.

"Aye, I do. And I think that's prudent. I don't see well enough for drivin' at night."

"One last question," Nora said. "Have you ever found a boot lying around?"

"A boot?"

"In places where it shouldn't be."

Erma shook her head.

"Can't say that I have."

Taking her tea, Nora went to her office. When she arrived, she looked at the window. On the sill stood a coal-black raven, its black eye trained on her.

She stopped in her tracks. For some reason, the bird unnerved her. Her hands trembled. The sudden urge to flee coursed through her veins, but she was frozen. As she watched, the raven opened its beak, as if speaking. Then, it flapped its wings and lifted into the morning sky.

Nora didn't move until her computer "beeped" its incoming mail sound.

Chapter Eight- The Message

The email reminded Nora that her meeting would start in ten minutes. She logged onto the meeting site and prepared her presentation. The process took longer than usual because her trembling fingers didn't find the keys as readily as normal. Still, the work was beneficial. She forced herself to focus on NIGHT OF THE DEAD instead of Hellfleet and Elija Ravenwood. The online meeting lasted for two hours, and it was approaching lunch time when it ended. Grabbing her cup, Nora started for the kitchen. She was ravenous.

Bowl of soup?" Erma asked.

"Sounds wonderful," Nora answered.

Taking a seat at the table, Nora pulled out her phone and reviewed her texts. Most were from Felix, and they were both informative and dear. She knew he was making time for her. She answered the texts and assured him all was well at Hellfleet — even if it wasn't. The last thing she wanted was to make him worry.

As Nora stirred the soup to cool it, Erma left for the day. Nora, surprisingly felt a pang of disappointment.

Work is work I suppose.

It wasn't just that she enjoyed having Erma around. Erma had her feet on the ground and Nora found her solid personality calming. Looking up from her phone, she spotted the bird, the raven, perched on a window sill. *Was it giving her the evil eye?* This one took flight immediately, making Nora feel better. She thought that now that she knew the story from Erma's perspective, the birds would lose their fear factor. *Really, what harm could birds do?*

As the first wave of rain slashed the windows, she added a dollop of whiskey to her tea and headed for her office. She really needed to relax a bit. Feeling a bit warmer for the whiskey, she plopped into her chair and tapped a key. The screensaver was quickly replaced by a message.

The words VEUVE AMIOT filled the screen.

~~~~~

For a moment, Nora couldn't believe her eyes. She blinked several times, wondering how the words came to be on her screen. She had no idea what the words meant, but she was pretty sure the message hadn't been generated by the computer. It was nothing she could ever remember seeing or hearing. What the bloody hell was Veuve Amiot?

She began to shake. Automatically, she looked over her shoulder, half expecting to find... well, she didn't quite know, what she had expected to find. The room was empty, the door empty. Whoever had left the message wasn't around to see her reaction. *Wait, was she alone?* Erma was gone. *Wasn't she?*

THE HAUNTING OF HELLFLEET POINT LIGHTHOUSE

Nora was near to tears. Someone or someone was messing with her. *Well maybe. But couldn't it just be a virus on the computer?*

Feeling emboldened by her logic, Nora put her fears to bed.

She would search, and assure herself, no one was here. And if they were… She grabbed her mug and stood up.

Searching the cottage was easy and quick. She found no one. For a moment, she considered climbing through the tower to check the lamp room, but with the storm, she didn't find that appetizing. It would be slippery and blustery up there. Instead, she locked the door to the tower.

Satisfied she was alone in the cottage, she returned to her office. She had no sooner found her chair before the fishy, seaweedy smell wafted around her.

It was the same seaweed odour as before, but that couldn't be. The hairs on Nora's neck rose up as a gnawing feeling entered her belly. *Please don't let it be.* Standing slowly, she made her way to the spare bedroom and came to an abrupt halt.

In front of her was the trunk lying open, and one worn, brown boot sat on the bed. Nora's legs felt like jelly and her breath, sounded ragged and loud.

How could that be? She had just checked the room, and everything had been in its place. No one was in the cottage with her, she had searched, and the only person with a key was Erma. Another explanation wormed into her brain. *Woody*, a small voice whispered inside her head. *Woody is here.* She shivered from head to toe.

She started to back away but stopped. The air had cleared, the smell was gone. She walked over, picked up the boot, and, tentatively put it to her nose, and sniffed.

No smell. But that still didn't explain what it was doing out of the trunk.

Angry, she stuffed the boot back into the trunk. Furious, she shoved the trunk under the bed and stormed from the room. She marched into the middle of the big room. She looked around as rain hammered the windows.

"I DON'T KNOW WHO YOU ARE," she shouted. "BUT I WILL BE BLOODY WELL DAMNED BEFORE I LET YOU CHASE ME FROM MY HOME! I'M WARNING YOU. WHEN I FIND YOU, AND I WILL, I'M GOING TO MAKE SURE YOU NEVER BOTHER ANYONE ELSE AGAIN!!"

Although the shouting made her feel better, she wasn't certain it had done any good. She had no way to punish a ghost, did she?

She ran to her office. She slid into her seat and stared at the screensaver wondering what to do. As she wondered, the screen saver refreshed. Long columns of VEUVE AMIOT filled all three screens. Nora opened her mouth and screamed.

Chapter Nine- Nora's Decision

After a moment, and nothing more had happened, Nora retrieved the whiskey bottle from the cabinet. She placed it on her work table and cleared the screens. Then, she quickly did an Internet search on Veuve Amiot.

What did a 1930s champagne have to do with this old lighthouse?

It was a good champagne with a world-renowned poster, and that was all it was. Nothing better than a dozen other champagnes from the era. So, why would someone fill her screens with its name? She grabbed the whiskey and turned away.

Outside, the worst of the storm had passed, leaving a light rain that she guessed would soon end. She sipped whiskey directly from the bottle and tried to work out what was happening and why.

If Woody were real, if he haunted the place, what connection did he have to a champagne from before the second world war? That didn't make sense. And if he wanted to, wouldn't he just try to kill her.

Maybe he was trying. She'd slipped on a fish and hurt her head *ON A FISH – A FISH ON THE FLOOR OF AN UNUSED BEDROOM.* Perhaps, now he was just messing with her mind.

Of course, it could be that she was cracking up, taking a walk off the deep end, losing it in some fashion. Perhaps the game had seeped into her psyche and was creating visions that weren't there. Perhaps, she had pulled the boot from the trunk and left it so she could find it and become frightened afresh. Without Felix around, how could she ensure that she was in touch with reality? Was she going mad? She put down the bottle and pushed away from the table. Nora didn't believe the answer was in the computer or the Internet. The answer was somewhere else, and she didn't have a clue as to where it might be. She pushed to the table again, printed out an image of the Vevue Amiot poster, and left the room.

Dusk arrived as Nora drove to St. George. After parking, she splashed her path through the myriad of puddles to the pub. Grabbed a pint on her way past the bar; Duncan winked in greeting. She slid into a booth and waited. She didn't wait long before Duncan joined her.

"Back for more?" Duncan asked.

"Let's suppose," Nora began. "Let's suppose that Hellfleet is really haunted. The question becomes how do we un-haunt it?"

Duncan rubbed his red nose and closed one eye, as if thinking.

"I don't know of anyone who ever tried to 'un-haunt' Hellfleet. I mean, I don't know of anyone who brought in a priest or something."

At that moment, Erma ambled into the pub. Nora spotted her and stood.

"Erma! Over here."

Duncan stood and allowed Erma to slide into the booth. Even as she did, the barmaid delivered ale for Duncan.

"You trying to take the girls money off her?" Erma quipped. "You're a cunning one, sly as a fox, got her thinking and talking about those old wives' tales, so she'll come back here and buy you a pint for the rest of the night."

"I pass on only what I've heard my whole life" Duncan protested. "I don't make up a single adjective, verb, or noun."

"All right, all right," Nora interjected. "Let's get past all that. As I was asking Duncan, what if Hellfleet is haunted? What do we do about it?"

"So, you've come to that conclusion?" Erma asked.

"It's either haunted, or you're trying to drive me out for some reason."

"I have no reason to drive you anywhere," Erma said, her face drawn up indignantly. "In fact, having someone in the Fleet makes me quid."

Duncan gave a smug smile, "Well, you'll have to admit that I'm – and –she," he pointed his finger at Nora, "is right, won't you Erma? And, as far as I know," Duncan added. "No one is clamorin' to move into Hellfleet. And for what it's worth" he continued, "I don't think old Erma would drive you out."

Erma, huffed. "Well at least you're right about that."

Nora ignored the antics.

"Then, there's a presence. How do we get rid of it?"

Erma and Duncan looked at each other and then at Nora.

"I suppose we have to determine what this... spirit wants," Duncan said.

"If you ask me," Erma said. "I think you need some sort of religious intervention. Maybe the pastor can drive it out."

Nora picked up her glass and sipped. She wasn't yet convinced she needed an exorcist. She had a ghost, not a demon. If she could figure out what it wanted, perhaps it would leave her in peace.

"What would Woody want with an old, brown boot and Vevue Amiot champagne?" she asked.

Erma and Duncan both frowned, and Nora understood that they didn't know about the boot.

For the next hour, Erma, Duncan, and Nora discussed Hellfleet, Ravenwood, and the brown boot. Nora heard more stories about cheeky ravens and frigid drafts on the hottest summer days and the cries of drowning sailors. But neither Erma nor Duncan had ever heard of a brown boot or the champagne. As far as they knew, the Wipford wasn't carrying any wine or spirits, just silk and tea. At the end, though, Nora seemed no closer to a solution then before. The only agreement between the three was that perhaps the ghost wanted something or needed something.

"Sometimes, spirits can't rest until they're whole," Erma said.

"I've heard of the ghosts of soldiers who roam the fields of battle looking for an arm or leg or head perhaps." Duncan's eyes were as round as saucers and glazed from beer.

"You old fool," Erma said. "Woody didn't lose his head that night."

"I was just givin' a what if," Duncan answered.

"Something that is lost inside Hellfleet?" Nora asked.

"Where else could it be?" Duncan looked from one to the other, "be no reason to haunt ya if it weren't there."

"I've cleaned the Fleet for years," Erma said. "I can't say I've ever seen anything there that would please a ghost."

"How do you know what would please a ghost?"

Nora downed the rest of her ale and held out her hands.

"Wish me well. If there's something there to find, I'll find it."

They shook her hand, and Nora left Erma and Duncan in the booth. That they were carping at each other didn't seem unnatural.

Back at Hellfleet, Nora knew she had had too much ale for an intelligent search. After checking her phone and answering texts, assuring Felix that all was well, she filtered through her emails, deleting those that weren't important and marking the ones that needed to be answered in the morning. That done, she went to bed.

If the scent of seaweed encased her or some frigid air wafted over her, she didn't notice. She slept without waking until bright sunshine filled the room and disturbed her. Eyes barely open, she spotted the bird sitting on the comforter.

Chapter Ten- The Search for the Secret

Nora recoiled, screamed and pushed herself away from the bird.

It jumped up and landed on the window sill for just a moment before taking flight. Nora breathed deeply, grateful that today was one of Erma's days and Nora wouldn't be alone. Maybe she would even help her search. She pushed the covers aside and climbed out of bed, hoping the kettle had just boiled.

But it hadn't. The kitchen was empty and Erma was late. Nora was surprised, but then again, Erma had imbibed a fair number of pints last night. That probably slowed her down. It really didn't matter, Nora would hunt for whatever the ghost wanted, on her own. Dressed and armed with a cup of tea, she set about searching Hellfleet.

~~~~~

Obviously, what she needed to find was hidden but hidden where? It had to be someplace not cleaned or seen on a regular basis, somewhere, not meant to be easily found. Looking around the main room her eye caught the window seat.

It had a solid base that sounded hollow when she tapped it. Wasn't it a perfect hiding place?

On her knees, Nora felt the entire base, seeking a seam or release of some kind. And she found one. She smiled as a heretofore hidden door opened. She reached into the space and felt around. Her fingers touched cloth.

Cloth? What she pulled from the space were several old, plaid blankets, the kind people used on cold, blustery evenings.

Blankets? What are they stuffed in there for?

She didn't know why someone would shove old blankets in a hidden cupboard. Perhaps, whoever it was, had been short on space, the lighthouse wasn't all that big if you were a hoarder. But she didn't see where blankets would help her. She placed the blankets on the kitchen table and went back to searching.

For the next two hours, Nora tapped every cabinet, every closet, and every place she thought might house a hidden space. She found absolutely nothing. She went to the blankets on the table and spread them out. They were just blankets, nothing more. Could a few old blankets be the explanation? She had searched everywhere, could there be anywhere else?

Her eye caught a flock of ravens soaring and dropping and soaring again; catching the wind for fun. Then, she thought of something. She hadn't explored the tower, had she? Was there anything there? She looked at the spiral staircase and made her way towards it.

Remembering that Ravens were usually sitting out on the platform, the climb seemed longer and harder than she remembered, she hated to admit it, but she was scared now.

Erma's talk about cheeky ravens was one thing, but since Erma had almost grudgingly admitted there could be a ghost she didn't trust the ravens so much anymore.

Poking her head into the lamp room and looking all around, she half expected the flock of them to land on the railing outside. But none did. What she hadn't noticed before was that the lamp in the tower rested on a short pedestal. While the pedestal looked solid, a thought popped into her mind. Perhaps it wasn't.

She went to her knees once more and examined the pedestal. It took less than a minute to find the door, and less than a minute more before she found the wooden box. When she pulled it out, she was amazed.

The narrow, long box with its rusted clasp looked like something from another century. She opened it and found a cover of red velvet. She pulled aside the velvet, and there it was.

A dusty bottle of Vevue Amiot champagne.

~~~~~

Nora picked up the bottle and blew off the dust. It was a 1939 vintage, and she had no idea if it was still drinkable. Frankly, it didn't matter. This looked like something that a spirit would wish uncovered, mostly because of its name and the fact that the same name was one that appeared on her screen.

"Is this it Woody?" She whispered, then she spotted the note in the box.

Picking it up she read five names on a short list. Three names had been lined through.

One was Wesley Archer, the other was Floyd Taylor, the late owner of the lighthouse. She wondered if his name needed to be lined out also. Erma was dusting when Nora returned from the tower. "Oh, you're here," Nora said. "I wanted to thank you for your patience with Duncan… and with me."

"Patience! With Duncan!" She gave a scoff. "He's always good for a yarn if there's a drink in it, but I wouldn't drive ya out and he knows it. And if somethings going on here, then I'd have to admit he might be right, wouldn't I? I might be old, but I'm not so stubborn as to being stupid. What have you there?"

Nora showed Erma the box and the contents. "What do you think? Is this what Woody's after?"

Erma looked at the list and gave a shake of her head with the assurance of one who knows. "That would be Floyd's."

"How do you know?"

"Well look at the year girl. Woody was a ghost long before that was a brew!"

"Right, of course." Nora blushed at her lack of detective skills and agreed. "Floyd's. Of course. As were the boots. Do you think Floyd could be the ghost?"

"Wouldn't think so. Floyd had nothing to do with the birds. They bothered him too."

"Perhaps this name here, this… Wesley Archer can shed some light."

"Maybe, I hope so, because it's a mystery to me."

~~~~~

64

When Nora entered her office, box in hand, she found her computer screens empty. Smiling, she looked up and held the bottle high.

"Here goes," she muttered quietly. Attacking the keyboard with newfound enthusiasm Nora searched. If Wesley Archer existed, she was going to find him.

Twenty minutes later, she called out to Erma, "I've found him,"

She grabbed her car keys.

"I'll likely be gone when you come back," Erma answered.

"Just lock the door."

As Nora slid behind the wheel, she patted the box resting on the next seat. Taking out her phone, she put in Wesley Archer's address into her GPS locator.

~~~~~

"I've been expecting you," Wesley Archer rasped.

Nora smiled at the frail, old man sitting in a worn wheelchair. She pulled up a seat and cradled the wooden box in her arms.

"You're the third Wesley Archer I've found," she said.

"And the oldest I'm sure."

His watery eyes were on her, but she wasn't at all sure he really saw her. They didn't seem focused. He wore a white tee and a striped robe that was meant for a larger man. New slippers covered his feet. Well, not new, just unused. She wondered how long he had been confined to the chair.

"You deserve a story," he said. "I need to make a claim, right?"

"If you wish," she answered.

"It's about the only thing I still remember. Funny how that is. Don't know if I had lunch, but I remember nineteen forty-four."

Wesley paused, and his eyes closed. Nora wondered if he was going to sleep. Then, his eyes opened.

"We went in on D-Day," Wesley continued. "The five of us looked out for one another as we broke out and chased the Jerrys across France. But we got a bit too far ahead. When they counter-attacked, we were trapped. We were pretty sure we were going to die, even after the old farmer shoved us into a dry cellar. It was only a matter of time. That was before we found the champagne. You can imagine what a bunch of soldiers looking at death did next. We opened a bottle because we weren't going to live anyway. At least, we would go out happy."

A tear slipped from his eye and ran unnoticed down his cheek.

"I don't know if you understand just how maudlin drunk soldiers can become. With death walking all around us, we figured we should do something special in case some of us made it. So, we grabbed the best bottle we could find and formed a pact. We would take the bottle back with us, and we would pass it around as we died. The last man would drink the bottle as a tribute to his fallen friends."

He looked apologetically at Nora

"I know how melodramatic that sounds. Cliché, I suppose. But it seemed like the thing to do. When you're young, you think things will never change. You'll always be young and laughing. Doesn't quite work out that way. I'm sure you know that even if you don't believe it." Nora smiled. She understood what he was talking about. Would she remain friends with the people she knew today? Not all of them.

"Can I see it?" he asked. She opened the case and pulled aside the velvet. He stared at the bottle as another tear chased the first. His shaking hand reached out and stroked the bottle, as if it were some sort of pet. She held out the list, and he shook his head.

"I don't read much any-more. Do you mind?"

"Not a bit." She unfolded the note. "Russell Dobson."

"Billy didn't make it back. He was the first. Mortar round got him. If we had had time, we would have mourned him. Death can't be contemplated in a war zone."

"Flynn Clements."

"Flynn had the best blonde hair in the regiment. Blue eyes too. In every village we liberated, the women swarmed him. Most of them wanted him to take them back to England. Even war-torn England was better than France. Flynn came home and married an heiress, an older woman. He would invite me and Floyd out to the summer house. We would drink champagne and rehash our brushes with death. After a while, we stopped going, and he stopped inviting. Life no longer accommodated drink and memory. Flynn was on a transatlantic cruise to New York when he fell overboard. They never recovered the body."

"Giles Holloway."

"He hated the name Giles. We used his middle name Robert. He was Bobby all the way. He was from a poor family up north, miners. That was not for Bobby, not after the war. He jumped on a boat and sailed to India. He made some money, but India was in turmoil. He would send us postcards. From there, he went to Saudi Arabia where he worked in the oil fields. I guess that mining background came in handy. He made money there too. From there to South America. Oil fields. I don't think he ever married, although he might have been married in every country he visited. He got sick in Caracas, very sick, and came back to England. I remember the last time I saw him. We were in a pub, talking old times. He asked who had the bottle, and I told him Floyd. That made him feel better, because he knew Floyd would keep the bottle safe. A week later, he died. Liver, I think."

"Floyd Taylor."

Wesley's lower lip trembled, and another tear seeped from his eye. He motioned to the table next to him, and Nora grabbed a tissue. He dabbed at his eyes with palsied fingers and took as deep a breath as he could manage.

"Floyd was the best of us. I don't say that because he won the cross. He deserved that if ever a soldier did.

He was braver than any person I've ever known."

He stopped for a moment in far-away memories. Nora waited a moment before speaking

"Go on, I'd like to hear more."

"Floyd was the one that held us together that day in France. And he was the one who took control of the bottle. On our anniversary—that's what we called it—on that day, we -all who remained- would get a note from him. He would tell us if someone had passed, and he would remind us of our duty. He was big on duty. I doubt Floyd could rest peacefully if he failed in his duty. He was the only man I would trust with my wife and my money. I owe my life to him. And I wish, I wish it was him who was going to drink the bottle. How did he…"

"You knew he lived in a lighthouse? He fell off the platform. A stroke or seizure, something like that."

"I suspected as much. Floyd wasn't one to live on the backs of others." Wesley slapped his wheelchair. "Or to be ferried around either."

Nora folded the note, slid it into the case, and placed the case in Wesley's lap.

"It seems you are the rightful owner."

"Would you partake of a glass with me?"

Nora smiled.

"I would be honoured."

Nora actually had two glasses, and while it wasn't the best tasting wine she had ever had, it was perhaps the most satisfying. When she left, Wesley was snoring softly. As she drove home, she wondered if she would ever have friends as close as those five men holed up in a dry wine cellar. She doubted it.

When she walked into the lighthouse, she felt a happy glow, the kind of glow she experienced whenever she completed a project.

She sat alone at the kitchen table and looked out the window. At sea, she could see dark clouds scudding over the horizon. A storm. While she didn't relish storms, she wasn't going to let it ruin this moment. She had completed Floyd's mission, and she was pleased.

"I did it," she said out loud. "I delivered the Veuve Amiot. You can rest now, Floyd. Your job is finished. And you know, I think I'm every bit as satisfied as you must be. Good bye, go on to where ever you're meant to be now."

Then, the scraping began.

Nora froze.

Chapter Eleven-
Paranormal Demands

"No, no, no, no, NO!" Nora shouted. "I did exactly what you wanted. You can't start this now. I delivered the champagne. Your commitment is over! GO, you can go. Please."

But the scraping didn't stop. In fact, it seemed louder. She jumped to her feet, grabbed her keys, and headed for the door. She had no idea where she was going, but she was certain she was going somewhere. If it wasn't about the champagne, then what was it about? She climbed into her car and started the engine. Before she could put the car in gear, she looked up. That's when she saw the open window.

An open window? In the lamp room? How in the world... No one had been up there except for her.

"FLOYD" she shouted. "WHAT ELSE DO YOU WANT?"

She glanced past the lighthouse to where the storm gathered. It didn't look like a gentle rain. It looked like a downpour, and a downpour might ruin the lamp room. Was it really a ghost? Was any of this a ghost? "Oh Felix" she cried to herself, "I'm losing it." She longed for him to come home quickly. Thoughts hammered at her mind.

How had that window opened? I could have sworn it was closed. Shutting off the engine, she headed back to the cottage. She didn't know what to do about anything, but she did know she was still going to leave at least for tonight — as soon as she closed that bloody window.

Inside, she remembered to lock the door behind her. Beside herself with disappointment, she marched doggedly through the breezeway and into the tower. As she climbed, the scraping increased, and a blast of cold air rushed over her.

"I'm bloody coming," she called, not caring anymore.

Then, there it was. That fishy, seaweedy odour now surrounded her, and she breathed through her mouth. It was as if Floyd was throwing everything he had at her. Did he want her to keep searching for something else? She didn't think that was it. She thought he wanted her to know that he hadn't left. Hot tears of rage fell from her eyes. She had no idea what to do next.

~~~~~

The lamp room was colder than Nora thought possible. The wind poured through the open window. As she shut the window, a raven appeared out of the dark and landed on the platform, she jumped back.

"What the bloody hell," she shouted.

If the first raven was surprising, the second was terrifying. It landed next to the first, the wind ruffling their feathers. It was as if they were daring her to come out. Nora bit her knuckle before she screamed.

"ENOUGH! ENOUGH! NO MORE RAVENS. DO YOU UNDERSTAND? NO MORE RAVENS!"

As if Floyd had heard her, the wind paused, and the ravens flew off. She didn't watch where they went. She didn't want to know. She backed up against the lamp and faced the storm.

And then, she had a thought. What if more than one ghost had haunted Hellfleet? What if Floyd had gone and Woody was here. Did he want to hurt her? She hoped not.

"OK," she said shakily, "I'm here. I'm right where you want me — I think. What now? Is that you Woody? If it is, I've decided to sell, I'll leave today. I know what I said earlier, about finding you, and all of that... but I've changed my mind. And, if it's you Floyd, then I'm still leaving. OK?"

Nora stood still, for a moment, not daring to move. Not knowing what would happen. Nothing happened. She turned to leave and took a step. It only took a few more steps before the noise started up.

The scraping came from outside the tower room. Nora stifled a sob. The storm seemed to pick up energy and battered at the doors and windows.

"What do you want?" she whispered.

A window behind her popped open, and she spun. Without thinking, she ran around and latched the window closed. It popped open again. Her body shivered, not so much from the cold but from the knowledge that whoever was here, wanted her out on the platform.

The breeze picked up again and buffeted her toward the door.

"Please, don't make me," she protested. The scraping jumped a notch in volume, and the cold almost made her teeth chatter. "Oh, God," she said stepping out onto the platform wondering what would come next. The wind whistled past her ears and whipped her face. As the door clicked shut, the first wave of cold rain lashed her, half soaking her.

Wouldn't it be better to race out of the place and at least try to get away? Not everyone had died, some had managed to leave. If she wasn't careful the wind would blow her off the platform anyway. The rain and wind were thrashing her around on the wire mesh.

She told herself that the first order of business was to get out of the wind. Holding onto the railing, she scooted around the platform. In the wind and torrents, she failed to see the raven in her way. When her foot hit it, she jumped. Her feet slipped on the wet mesh, and she slid under the railing.

Her fingers raced along the cold metal as her grip failed, and she knew she would soon plunge to her death many metres below. Her hands reached out and found a vertical support. With a huge effort, she wrapped one arm around the support and swung up her legs. Luckily, her legs found the metal support underneath the mesh, and she quickly wrapped her thighs around it.

Everything seemed to come to a halt as she clung to the supports. The wind howled, driving rain into her eyes, blinding her. And while she was safe for the moment, she knew the wet and the cold would soon sap her strength. She couldn't hang on long. A bolt of lightning lit up the lighthouse, and she glimpsed a spot of red around the bottom of the support.

A high-pitched sound on the wind reached her ears.

What could that possibly be? Nora's heart almost stopped. *Was it the scream of the sailors that she heard?*

Was she going to fall to her death and meet them?

Gripping on for dear life, tears began streaming down her face. She was too confused to make any sense of this at all.

More lightning flashed and illuminated the surface below her. A flash of red glinted and she knew for certain that something was lodged in a gap at the bottom of the support. What difference did that make? She was battling for her life. Whatever that was, it would have to wait.

At that moment, the support slipped. Not a big slip, a tiny slip, but even so a slip and her body lowered a little... if the support failed... She didn't finish the thought. Being closer now, when the next flash came, she could see that the red was attached to some kind of metal.

Confused, desperate, and beside herself with fear, Nora did the only thing she could think to do. Holding on with one hand, she bent down and felt around the support. Her fingers found cloth, and she tugged. The thing didn't want to come out. She jerked, and it came free.

There was an instant, when she swung away from the support and the platform, but she fought and managed to hang on. She didn't bother looking at what she had found. She shoved it into her pocket and grabbed the platform again.

"OK, FLOYD OR WOODY, OR WHOEVER THE HELL YOU ARE, IF THIS IS WHAT YOU WANT, I'VE GOT IT!"

Nothing happened.

Nora blinked the water from her eyes and fought to keep her grip despite the cold. Her fingers were beginning to cramp, and her whole body shook in the awful cold. At that moment, the raven landed on her arm.

She couldn't believe it. How had the bird made it through the storm? Why was it there? Even as she watched, it pecked her hands.

What the bloody hell?

She shouted and spat at the bird, but it simply looked at her and pecked again. This was insane. She screamed and it flew off, only to land again on her head.

PECK.

Nora swung herself around causing the support to slip a bit more. The bird simply sat there.

"IF YOU WANT WHAT I HAVE, GET RID OF THIS BIRD OR SO HELP ME I'LL THROW THIS THING INTO THE SEA AND YOU'LL NEVER FIND IT!"

At that moment, the raven flew away. A bright light flooded the platform. Nora stared, the lighthouse lamp had come alive, something that wasn't possible. At least, she thought it was the lamp. It couldn't be lightning because lightning was like a photographer's flash.

No, this was a very bright light that lasted seconds, the seconds she needed to spot a grip in the platform mesh. She had never noticed the gaps before, the perfectly spaced gaps. She flung her hand over the side and slid her fingers into the hold and pulled.

Half her protesting body slid onto the platform as the light focused on another hold. She threw her other hand like a mountain climber and found the spaces. Another hoist, and she was atop the platform, panting and shivering.

Then, the light vanished.

She was once again in the dark and cold and wet. Coughing, sobbing, she crawled to the door, praying that it hadn't locked behind her. Half frozen fingers clawed at the latch and managed to open the door. She fell inside and kicked the door shut. Sobbing, aching from cold, soaked from head to toe, she began to laugh. She had almost died, except for something in her pocket, something a ghost wanted, and she laughed hysterically.

Chapter Twelve- The Reluctant Ghost

"What is this?" Erma asked.

"The Victoria Cross," Nora answered. "Floyd's Victoria Cross."

Erma handed back the medal.

"Never seen one of them before."

"Me either."

"Where did you find it?"

"Under the platform around the lamp room."

"Last night?"

She nodded.

"What possessed you?"

"I think Floyd wanted me to get this. And I almost didn't. The raven didn't want me to. But after I found it, the odours and drafts and sounds stopped."

"And the ravens?"

"I think they are gone too. But I'm not sure."

Erma poured herself a cup of tea and started for the bedrooms.

"I'll change the sheets if you wish."

"Thank you."

Nora watched Erma disappear before she picked up the cross. If Floyd wanted her to retrieve it, then she thought she knew what to do with it.

~~~~~

Nora watched as Wesley turned the cross over and over in his arthritic hands. She knew Wesley's watery eyes couldn't see the cross. She suspected that he was more than half blind. Still, she wasn't about to question him. If Wesley said it was Floyd's, then by all that was holy, it was Floyd's.

"He was fond of it, wasn't he?" Nora said.

"More fond than I can say."

"What did he do?"

"He tried to get himself killed is what he did. You don't charge a machine gun nest and live to tell about it. I was among those that survived because of what he did."

"So, you want to keep the cross?"

Wesley shook his head. "It's not mine, and while I cherish Floyd's memory, this should be with him. You knew he had his own special ceremony, didn't you?"

"No, what?"

"Every VE day he had one."

"OK. What did he do?"

"On Victory in Europe day, he would put on his uniform, pin on his cross, and salute London. He was mad about that."

"So, what should I do with it? The grave?"

"I can't see another place for it."

He handed back the cross and smiled, exposing mostly toothless gums.

"Thank you for bringing it to me, and thanks again for sharing the champagne. I think I can go now."

Nora put the cross in her purse and touched the old man's hand.

"I don't think Floyd had a better friend."

She left him with a smile on his face.

A bright sun made the cemetery more hospitable. Nora wound her way through the headstones. She found Floyd's grave which was not yet grown over. She stopped to read the simple headstone. Nothing more than name and dates. For some reason, she thought he deserved more. He had saved a bunch of soldiers from certain death, and he should be recognized for that, if for nothing more.

She knew that when Wesley passed on, there would be virtually no one who would know what a hero Floyd had been.

Kneeling down she took the cross from her purse looking at it a moment before she began to dig. She didn't dig deep, just a few inches, just deep enough to ensure the medal would remain. She covered the hole and stood.

"That's it, Floyd. We're done, I hope. I think this is what you wanted all along. Rest in peace."

Nora executed an awkward salute and turned to leave. She walked quickly, brushing a happy tear for Floyd away. He could go now, and she had a game to finish.

~~~~~

Dusk had arrived by the time Nora reached Hellfleet Point. As she parked, she looked up. Strange, there appeared to be a light on in the lamp room. She hadn't expected that. Nor had she expected to find an open window in the cottage when she entered. For a moment, she wasn't sure about what was going on.

"Floyd, is it you? What's wrong. Why can't you leave." A long sigh of exasperation blew from her lips and she massaged her temples.

From somewhere came a soft, quavering rendition of GOD SAVE THE QUEEN. As it faded, she understood that maybe Floyd needed something more but why the lamp room again? She passed through the cottage to the tower and started up.

Then, it hit her, the unmistakable smell. It was so strong she could taste it.

Chapter Thirteen- Attack of the Ravens

Nora almost choked as the taste of old fish seemed to regurgitate in her throat. Nausea swirled in her stomach and she wondered if she would throw up. All she wanted to do was to fly up the stairs and breathe in the fresh air from the tower. It would be cleaner up there, at least the gusts would blow the smell away.

Trying to ignore the salty rancid taste, she made her way up the stairs. Once at the top she heard screams on the wind. The taste of rotten fish was strong in her throat, and she spat it out.

"Floyd, what's going on?" she whispered.

A cold dark presence surrounded her. Whether it was in her head, or it was actually there she couldn't be sure. But sinister thoughts entered her mind. *I will die tonight.* Once the thought had formed, a dreadful vision played out in her mind, one where she tumbled from the tower to lie still and broken on the rocks. Panicking she tried to retreat from the stairwell, but fear had made her legs immobile. She heard her own screams sounding on the wind, and from somewhere far away, other tortured screams joined her, wailing in sorrow.

And that was when she realised. *This is not Floyd*. Floyd didn't moan, he sang. She'd heard it, even tonight. The tales of sailors screaming on the wind was only ever attributed to the ghost called Woody. And so was the noxious odour. And that happened long before Floyd ever arrived at the lighthouse.

The malevolence was palpable, she almost felt it salivating. Then Nora understood.

She understood what Duncan and the townsfolk didn't. This was not a ghost seeking vengeance. It was much more than that. She was right that there were two spirits here. But it wasn't Woody. The other, was the ghost of the wrecker. The spirit that confronted her here was sadistic and murderous. A wrecker of ships and lives; an evil opportunist.

The shock of the revelation jolted her to action, she fought the panic and flew back down stairs running for her life. The noxious smell surrounded her. A sadistic laugh rippled softly through her mind. Nora screamed.

"FLOYD? ARE YOU HERE? I NEED YOU."

A gust of wind blew down the stairs. The tower door was banging in rhythmic time with the strains of 'GOD SAVE THE QUEEN' which floated down to her.

Nora didn't want to go back up but Floyd was there and he would help her. Sobbing she started back up the stairs reasoning that it didn't matter where she went, the spirit of the malicious wrecker was surrounding her and she knew it wouldn't let her leave. It would kill her one way or another. Floyd was her only hope.

~~~~~

There was no light in the lamp room, just the last rays of the setting sun passing through the prism glass. The door to the platform stood open.

As she went to close it, she spotted the raven. It was easily the biggest raven she had ever seen.

Nora judged it to be three times the size of a normal bird. And in its beak, it held something. Nora's necklace. Passed onto her by her grandmother, with whom she shared the same birth month. A silver necklace with a large ruby stone.

Confused she wondered why the raven had it, and if this is what Floyd had wanted her to see.

She stared at the raven who stared back, as if daring her to come after it. Nora clutched at her neck, and felt the empty space. It usually sat in her jewel box when she wasn't wearing it. How the raven had come to be in possession of it, she couldn't begin to guess. But it didn't matter, she knew it was at the behest of the ghost. And this ghost killed for treasure.

A sickening feeling developed in the pit of her stomach. *It's not just treasure, it's a souvenir, the victory of another kill. Its taunting me.*

Holding her breath, Nora didn't know what to do.

The creature can have it. Why not? I'd be a fool to play games with a ghost who's trying to kill me.

But if it's going to kill me, I'll be damned if I just let it mock me as well.

"Floyd, what's going on? Why am I up here?"

The raven hopped closer to her, necklace dangling tantalisingly from its beak. She could almost reach it. Perhaps if she could grab that monstrous bird...

Nora eased out of the door, moving cautiously not wanting to spook it. But how could she spook a spook? The craziness of it made her laugh; she sounded manic. It didn't fly off.

Nora absently wondered if she was doing that thing that psychologists call dissociation. As she moved, the raven, necklace in beak, hopped away again.

"Don't be that way," she said out loud. "Just give me the necklace."

The bird merely eyed her for a moment before jumping a few more steps away.

Concentrating on the bird, Nora didn't realize that she had moved from the solid part of the platform around to the section where she had dangled and battled with the storm. She remained unaware of it until the raven jumped into the air.

For a moment, Nora thought to leap at the bird in a desperate attempt to grab it. But when the platform swayed under her feet, she stopped herself. Frozen on the spot, she barely dared to breathe. The platform creaked and groaned as an edge of it came away from the sides. Not knowing what to do, she stood there, the raven treading air as it were, a few meters above her.

Gritting her teeth, she wondered if this was the moment she was supposed to see her whole life flash in front of her. *Where are you Floyd?*

She looked around and she saw another side of the section that had separated and was hanging at an angle It was between her and the door.

Not trusting the section, she hugged herself into the glass and edged around the tower and toward the other side of the open door. But now, the back of it was facing her. She needed to somehow get around it, without going too far out on to the broken section of platform. If she could do that, she should be able to jump back inside.

She leaned against the door, trying to partly close it, but it didn't move.

Panic started to surface and she fought to keep calm. The door had to close, didn't it? She pushed harder. It didn't budge. She leaned out as far as she dared and looked. The problem was simple. When the platform came apart, the section by the door tilted and blocked it from closing, which blocked her from getting around it, and back inside.

She thought for a moment, wondering if she could climb onto the railing, hold onto the door, and jump. But when she actually touched the railing, she found it sickeningly unstable. She saw no way that it would hold her. Panic started to surface and she eased away from the door back against the glass of the tower.

In the scant light, she could see the sky was filled with ravens. They circled the tower as if waiting for her to fall. She could only guess what they would do to her, once splattered on the rocks below. She thought she heard the wrecker laugh again.

Then, she remembered her mobile.

She tugged the phone from her pocket and smiled at the ravens.

"Not yet," she said out loud. "Not yet." Even as she tapped, the ravens attacked.

Head down, Nora didn't see the birds coming. Two landed on her arms, pecking at her hands. Another landed in her hair, and she felt the talons grab and the beak peck. Startled, she dropped the mobile. It skidded across the mesh and slipped over the edge. She knew it had been destroyed on the rocks.

As soon as it disappeared, the birds flew off. She looked at her bleeding hands. She felt warm blood on her forehead. A hard breeze ruffled her hair. And the stench of seaweed encased her.

She pinched her nose and breathed through her mouth as the ravens flooded past her. She looked over, and the scene horrified her. The birds were congregating on the platform section next to the one where she stood.

As she watched, more birds landed, and as they landed, the unsupported section tilted. For a moment, she wasn't sure what was going on, but she soon realized that the sheer weight of the birds was separating the section from the rest of the platform.

Terror gripped her, and dizziness swirled in her head. Another bird landed and she screamed –

"NOOOOOOOOOOOOOOOO!!!" But it did no good.

The section pulled loose and plummeted, leaving almost a two-metre gap between her and the next section of the platform.

If ever Nora needed help, it was now. But who? In the soon to be dark, no one would see her. No one would hear her.

She was isolated, alone. And as she watched, the birds began to land on the next section. She stared, mesmerized, watching her last chance to survive being taken away.

Then, she heard it, or thought she heard it, that quavering version of GOD SAVE THE QUEEN.

"FLOYD!" Nora yelled. "HELP ME!"

The voice seemed right above her head. She looked up, and there dangled a boot, one of Floyd's boots.

It looked to be caught on a shingle or hook or something, but she didn't care. She grabbed the boot and stared at it. How would it help? She remembered Wesley, what he said about Floyd charging a machine gun nest. It was crazy. She looked from the boot to the birds.

With all her strength, she threw the boot at the birds. It hit some, scared many, and cleared the platform. Before the birds could mount another try, Nora backed up as far as she dared, took two quick steps, and leaped across the gap.

When she landed, the weakened section tilted under her weight. She slid backwards. Falling down, her hands searched for a hold... and she found two, one for each hand.

She dangled, afraid to try anything. Holding on, she felt the section stop moving. She was almost certain that she could pull herself onto the mesh. From there, it was a short crawl to the open door. All she had to do was pull.

Then, the huge raven landed.

The black gleam of the raven's eye challenged her. For a long second, it did nothing. Then, with ferocious speed it pecked her hand.

The beak sank into her skin, drawing blood, and while the pain was excruciating, she couldn't let go. She watched as the bird hopped and punctured her other hand. She screamed in panic and fury and despair.

Nora had no idea how it happened, but at that moment, with her hands bleeding, her strength ebbing, the raven getting ready for another attack, the boot fell from the sky.

It hit the raven squarely in the head, stunning the bird. It fell over, and Nora recognized her chance. She heaved herself onto the platform, safe for the moment.

Panting, she grabbed the boot. The raven stood up and shook itself off. Its beady, black eye trained on her, the raven spread its wings to fly. Nora knew she couldn't let it get away. She lunged and latched onto a leg with her left hand.

And the raven went crazy.

It immediately flew at her face, pecking, batting with its wings, sinking a talon into her hand. The sky in front of her turned black as other ravens flew at Nora scratching at her arm, landing in her hair. It was a full-scale attack, but something in her knew she couldn't lose. With the boot in her right hand, she hammered the huge raven.

Once, twice, three times before it fell over.

When it did, the other ravens flew off.

For a moment, she didn't know what to do. She wasn't sure if she could kill the bird no matter how many times she struck it.

And if she did, would that get rid of the wrecker? As doubt filled her mind, she heard it, those faint strains of GOD SAVE THE QUEEN.

A thought popped into her mind and she knew what to do.

She grabbed the bird and stuffed it into the boot, head first. It was a tight fit and halfway through the process the raven came alive, fighting her. But she didn't stop. She pushed until the bird was completely imprisoned inside Floyd's boot. Then, as quickly as her bloody hands could manage, she laced up the boot and tied it tight. Boot in hand, she stood.

"Now what?"

She looked out and decided. With all her strength, she slung the boot out over the rocks. It seemed to fly much further than her strength allowed, over the rocks and breakers, until it plopped into the cold ocean.

She watched for a moment to see if it would bob to the surface. It didn't. Floyd was taking his prisoner to the bottom of the sea. She looked around, and suddenly all the ravens took flight. As full dark storm clouds raced toward her, she limped around the swaying platform and through the door. She hadn't taken three steps before the entire platform pulled free. She reached out to pull the door closed, and she saw the mangled, ruined platform clatter to the rocks.

Shuddering, she eased her way down the stairs.

Chapter Fourteen- Floyd's Gift

Nora and Felix picked their way along the stones toward a large rocky outcrop.

'It's a good fishing spot', Erma had said. 'Floyd often caught a fish out there. He always give me one if it were spare.'

They weren't there to try their hand at fishing though. The old metal platform was in the process of being cleared away and the noise of it all drove them out of the cottage.

Nora's hands were still covered in deep scabs but since the event on the platform, there had been no fishy smells, no screams, no songs about saving the queen, or stray boots. Soon, there would be a solid new platform. Because neither of them wanted to lose access to the view. But mostly because a lighthouse with-out a platform, would be – just wrong.

"Are you disappointed about New York?" Nora asked, steadying her step with the help of Felix's arm.

"A little, but not too much." Felix's eyes told the truth. "The timings not right, and if setting up a New York office had been viable right now, then we'd be right back to city life again. Neither of us want that. There'll be other opportunities."

The waves washed up over the rocks, pulling the tide ever further back. Rock-pools glistened in the sun, their various occupants closing up tight or skittering away, when Nora stuck a finger in, indulging a childhood habit of touching almost everything in the shallow pools.

Felix was just a few steps ahead of her now. He had reached the rock outcrop. As he meandered there something glinted in the sun, catching his eye. At first, he thought it was a piece of sea glass, until he looked longer. Bending down, he picked up a batch of seaweed and began picking away the thick mass from what appeared to be a silver necklace with its stone still perfectly intact. Pulling it free, he turned to Nora, who was now at his side, and wondering what he was looking at. He showed her the necklace, pieces of seaweed still clinging to it.

"Oh, my Lord! I thought I'd lost it forever." Nora stared at it a long moment. She removed the debris before fastening it around her neck. Thinking of his Victoria Cross, she said "Thanks Floyd, we're even now."

By the time they reached the cottage grounds, the last of the trucks was driving off with its load of metal. Erma had arrived and was madly waving to them from the kitchen window.

The Beeb was playing loudly when they entered. "Sit down lovies." Erma chattered, "I think you'll like this. It's about that Wesley bloke you were looking for. The one with the champagne and letter."

The host's voice sounded out from the radio.

"The last remaining member of the Queens 100 fusiliers brigade, Wesley Archer, died recently at the age of 95. He was one of the party that assaulted Juno beach on D-day 1944. His passing signifies the end of an era. But one that ended happily for Wesley. Wesley recently received a bottle of 1939s Vevue Amiot champagne, passed around among a group of friends for decades. The wine was taken as a souvenir from the cellar of a French farmer. The farmer hid five men from German troops. We have his son Russell Archer here to tell us a bit about the story."

Erma poured tea and sliced a pound cake as the three sat comfortably together at the table. Nora nodded in agreement as she heard the tale, retold by Wesley's son. As Russell concluded the story, the radio host's voice chimed in at exactly the right moment.

"Thank you, Russell. You must be very proud of your father. We all are, for his service. I think it would be quite appropriate to honour Wesley with a rendition from the London army band and choir, of 'God Save the Queen'."

The sounds drifted out from the radio, clear and pure as a new morning.

With a soft quavering echoing in Nora's ear.

THE END

Thank-You for Reading

The Haunting of Hellfleet Point Lighthouse

I hope you enjoyed it and would very much appreciate

it if you could take a few minutes to

Leave A Review

Over the page you'll find previews of two of my other books

Here is Your Preview of The Haunting of Knoll House

Prologue

Knoll House
South Downs
West Sussex
United Kingdom
August 1992

Claire didn't believe the rumours, and she didn't see why anyone else should either. She rolled her eyes at the gasps she got when she told people what she was planning to do, and their warnings just made her more determined. At least, until Sarah refused to join her.

"You can't be serious," Claire said. They were sitting on Sarah's bed and Sarah was playing with a doll while avoiding Claire's eyes, both of which struck her as very childish – eleven was far too old for that sort of behaviour.

"You know what they say," Sarah said.

"I know the scary stories our parents use to keep us away from the place."

"Maybe there's a reason they want to keep us away."

"They probably just think it's unsafe because it's old and rickety. As if we can't take care of ourselves. Come on; imagine the looks on everyone's faces when we tell them what we did."

"I just don't think that's worth dying," Sarah said, now twisting the doll's hair especially roughly.

"Are you scared?"

"Yes."

"You do realise there's no such thing as ghosts?"

"Well I don't realise that because I've never seen a ghost so how would I know for sure?"

"Listen." Claire grabbed the doll and threw it on the floor, which made Sarah finally meet her eyes. "All the boys who say that we can't join in with them will have to shut their fat mouths when they find out what we did. When school starts we'll be *legends*. And we don't have to tell them when we find nothing – we can come up with all kinds of crazy stories about what happened in there. I mean, obviously we'll have to get them straight together so it all matches up and people believe us, but it's totally worth it. And I won't have anyone saying that Claire Anderson backs down from a dare. Never have, never will."

"That does not seem like a smart way to live your life" Sarah said parroting something her parents often said. "What if somebody dared you to jump off a cliff?"

Claire ignored this.

"Sarah, you didn't see the look on Dave's stupid face. He *wants* us to back out."

"*I* want us to back out," Sarah retorted. "And I never agreed to it so it wouldn't even be backing out anyway."

Technically Claire did not agree with that – given that she had already said Sarah would do it. But that was an unimportant detail.

"Please Sarah?" she said. "Do it for me. We go in, we take a few photos, we get out. What's–"

"Don't say 'what's the worst that could happen'," Sarah said. "Whenever people say that the worst *does* happen."

"Sarah," Claire leaned forward. "It'll be fine. There is no such thing as ghosts. In, out, legends. I promise we don't have to stay long and I *promise* it'll be worth it."

Sarah bit her lip. Claire had to smile at that. She knew it meant she had won. They waited until past midnight, telling each other stories to keep awake until Sarah's parents had gone to bed.

When they were sure they were asleep, Claire and Sarah snuck into the kitchen where Sarah's mother kept her camera then, with one last nervous glance at each other, they walked out into the cold night and headed for the house Knoll House, up on the windy hill.

Claire had to admit, as each step took them slightly closer to their destination, that she *was* a little scared. She tried to remind herself that was illogical and stupid; old empty houses were just that – empty. But it was hard to argue with years and years of ghost stories, and rumours, about the old mansion on the hill.

She was pretty sure her parents had grown up scared of the place and her grandparents and probably every generation back to the last one who had lived there.

But Claire believed in evidence. She had figured out Santa Claus wasn't real when she was three and she had never been the type to believe in anything she couldn't see with her own two eyes. It was that knowledge that made her push away every excuse.

It was too cold, they should wait until they had a better way of proving it, they should bring more people just so nobody could argue with what they had done. It would be so easy to find a reason to turn back and Sarah would agree without hesitation and despite promising that they definitely *would* go in the house at some point they'd probably never say another word about it and laugh at how silly and scared they were in ten years' time.

But that was the thing; that which separated Claire from generations of scared kids was a bull-headed determination. It made her keep walking, even as every shadow cast by a tree or streetlight started to look like skeletal arms reaching for them and the half-moon vanished behind lazily drifting dark clouds. The streetlights became sparser as they left the central part of the village and soon they were on the long, country road fringed with overgrown fields behind fences, the part of the village everyone liked to pretend didn't exist.

Any time she glanced at Sarah she could see, even in the darkness, how pale and terrified her friend was, and so she stopped glancing and locked her eyes on the road ahead. A couple of times she thought she saw Sarah, out of the corner of her eye, turn to her, mouth open, ready to ask if they could turn back. Maybe part of her wanted that to happen.

But Sarah never did and so they kept walking as the whistling wind picked up and the road slowly began to slope upwards.

A chill that had nothing to do with the weather came over Claire as she saw, in the distance at the top of the ever-steepening hill, the shape of the house. Why somebody every would have designed something so horrid, Claire couldn't say. Even in its prime it must have looked somewhat like an elongated skull.

Narrow windows overhung the dark maw of its veranda, the pillars seemed to hold it up like leering teeth, the only thing between them and the darkness beyond. Now the wood and stone were worn and grey, where once they had been painted brilliant white – something Claire was fairly sure could only have worsened the skull likeness.

A towering fence surrounded the house, but the hill meant that you could still see the whole bulk of it even from a distance, jutting up from the weeds and tangle of unkempt bushes that nobody ever did anything about. Over the years her parents had spoken idly of people who wanted to buy the place and fix it up, turn it into a bed and breakfast or the like, but that never seemed to happen. When Claire had been very small the almost permanent 'For Sale' sign that sat on the side of the road had been removed because, really, after so long what was the point anymore?

The best thing for the place would have been a visit from the wreckers, but nobody in this village could be bothered to go to those lengths, or maybe they were too scared to, and so Knoll House remained, terrifying everyone with the lingering belief that there was something inside you didn't want to disturb. Until tonight.

103

Feet from the fence, Claire and Sarah came to a halt. Claire's eyes scanned the distant building, focusing on the shape of it so as to keep her attention on anything but her beating heart. Beside her Sarah hugged herself, not saying anything. They must have stood there for at least ten minutes; both wanting to leave, neither wanting to say it. But Claire had made a promise to herself and she was not going to give up on that.

In under an hour they would be on their way back home, victorious, with a camera that proved there was nothing inside but cobwebs and dust. Then finally everyone could shut up about the haunted house and finally, maybe, the boys would let Claire join in their games.

"Are you ready?" Claire whispered.

Sarah didn't reply. Worried that looking at her would weaken her resolve, Claire decided to take her silence as a yes and so she started to walk. For a few seconds, she heard nothing behind her and worried that Sarah might refuse to come after all – what she would do in *that* situation she couldn't say – but then she heard footsteps and together they headed for a famous gap in the fence, one people tended to come up and look through but never enter.

She felt short of breath already and her heart was growing louder by the second, but passing the first threshold that was the gap seemed to have ignited a tiny flame of courage in her heart, a flame that let her smile knowing she was already braver than just about every kid who had ever tried to take this challenge. She turned to share her smile with Sarah, but one look at her friend's face made it clear that smiling was not on the agenda for her. Fair enough.

They kept walking.

The wind was picking up with every step, the dead trees and sprawling bushes rustling and shaking with increasing violence. Had Claire been more imaginative she almost could have fancied the sounds forming a voice. Go back, it said.

Go back now before it's too late. She laughed quietly and shakily. She *was not* scared.

'Go back'.

The voice was as clear as day, from right behind her. She spun, but Sarah was still walking, head down.

"Did you say something?" Claire had to try hard to keep the tremor out of her voice.

Sarah shook her head. "Please don't try to scare me," she said. "Let's just get this over with."

Claire's eyes moved past Sarah, but all she saw were the bushes and the weeds. She made to turn.

'Please.'

She spun again. Sarah had passed her now and the voice had definitely come from behind, pleading and desperate. It sounded like somebody who would do anything to stop this moment from happened. It sounded like the stupid fear Claire had pushed away since she was a kid, the fear that made her want to cry out for her parents every time she had an ugly nightmare, the fear that tried to drag her down and tell her she was just another weak little child.

No.

Claire refused to entertain stupid fantasies a second longer. She turned her attention fully to the house now, which loomed up above them, dark and shadowy and more like a skull now than ever. She let herself feel that fear then she put it away in a little box, locked it and threw away the key. No more.

She picked up her pace, passing Sarah and climbing the front stairs on to the veranda.

Rotting wood creaked and gave way slightly beneath her feet.

If that voice came again she couldn't say – she pushed everything away, everything except for the house.

She reached out and grabbed the rusted doorknob. It was ice cold. She looked back. Sarah had not come on to the veranda yet. She was frozen in front of the house, staring up at Claire, tears in her eyes.

For a moment they just stood there, looking at each other, as if a silent conversation was playing out. Claire turned the doorknob.

"Claire," Sarah said. Her voice was high pitched and cracking.

Claire paused.

"Please," Sarah said. "Please let's go home."

Claire pushed the door open and walked inside.

Chapter One - The Withered Town

London
United Kingdom
December 2017

She had gotten very drunk the night before; sitting by herself in a bar, knocking back whiskey after whiskey until she was kicked out and had to stagger home through the London streets. When her alarm went off that morning she wanted to smash it with a hammer, but even through her pain she knew that anger was more directed at herself than anyone else.

She had known she had an early start that day. Had known it for weeks now. But still, drinking was the only way she was going to get any sleep that night. It had been the only way she could sleep for days now, ever since she had made this decision.

She arrived at the station early, dragging her case behind her. After picking up her ticket she tried and failed to choke down a sandwich before spending ten minutes in the bathroom. wondering if she would to throw up. That sensation, she knew, probably had little to do with the hangover.

In the train windows, her reflection looked drawn and gaunt against the turbulent grey sky beyond.

Older than her twenty-six years. Although she had looked older than her years for a very long time now. Felt it too.

She tried to relax but knowing her destination made the journey impossible to enjoy. Simultaneously she wanted it to last forever and end quickly. Every slowly passing second was a tightening screw, albeit one that brought her closer to the things she had been running from for more than half of her life.

She dreaded the moment the landscape became familiar. The fields, orchards and rivers that surrounded the village where she had grown up had soured over the years; even the best memories curdling like off milk as the moment that had been the dividing line between then and now infected all of them. A slow cancer, moving outwards from the nexus point of one stupid, childish choice.

She leant her forehead against the cool glass and closed her eyes. It soothed her pounding head somewhat, although maybe that wasn't what she wanted. Maybe the real reason she had gotten so drunk last night, and the reason for all of those other nights and all of the other stupid things she had done, was the vague sense that she deserved it.

Was that masochistic, or just the smallest, most pathetic attempt to balance things out again? She supposed it didn't matter now. She opened her eyes and forced herself to watch the landscape change. Maybe she should have given London a grander goodbye. The city had been her home for a very long time after all. She had worked, studied, loved and lost there, made friends and planned a career all while that weight kept pulling her down until finally she had to roll the dice that would either cut it off for good or allow her to finally succumb to it. She wasn't even sure what she wanted more.

But, as the train moved, she knew that what really terrified her wasn't the ultimate destination of her trip.

It was everything that would come before that. Everything she had long since convinced herself she had escaped. The pointing fingers and accusing eyes, the forced smiles that tried to cover for all that hate and blame. Feeling like you deserved something did little to make you want to face up to *that*.

She had been on this train for a while now but the dread of familiarity had yet to shift into the awareness of it. She would have thought she'd have recognised the landscape by now. Or at least remember it from previous trips, because it was surprising that she could forget *this*. The grass was almost all dead in all directions, the orchards sparse and sad, bare tree branches reaching towards the grey sky as if begging for help. But not even the threatened rain could help this land. It looked dead and decayed, a long way from the green fields she knew so well.

But then...

She frowned. Something about the way those sad orchards lined up, the hills behind them and the placement of the fences *was* familiar, like a grey sketch of a famous painting. And that small cluster of houses looked a lot like the farm that marked the outskirts of her village and...

And in that moment Claire knew. She *was* home, and home was worse than she had dared suspect. The rot, it seemed, had not just permeated her life. As the train pulled into the village proper and she took in all those sights she had once known so well, a deep, hollow sadness took the place of niggling fear.

Once this village had been vibrant, pretty and somewhat quaint – the perfect place to retire or bring up your kids, the kind of English village that adorned postcards. Now it looked as though all the colour had been sucked out of it, taking with it the life.

The paint was faded, bricks were cracked and worn, streets uneven. Looking at it all framed against the grey sky it was hard to imagine that the sun ever shone here. Around her, other passengers had stopped looking out the windows, returning their eyes to their phones and books and newspapers, turning away because they *could* turn away from the bad place, could ignore this terrible feeling of *wrongness* and go on to their destination with only the barest prickle of an uncomfortable memory. They did not need to call this void home. They did not need to come back here to right a terrible wrong.

As the train pulled to a halt and she gathered her things, she wished with such acute pain that she could be one of these simple ignorant people, averting her eyes until the land was pleasant and the world made sense again. To be protected from the pain by those thick glass windows. She wasn't sure she had ever been so jealous of anyone. She had dressed warmly but the cold still bit to her skin as she stepped on to the otherwise empty platform. She ignored her momentary desire to jump back on to the train and stay there until she was far away from here. The moment to turn away was gone and there was no point regretting it. Claire Anderson was home.

The Haunting of Knoll House

Available at

http://a-fwd.com/asin-uk=B077ZRN1YZ

Here is Your Preview of The Haunting of Stone Street Cemetery

Chapter One - The Cemetery

"How many more of these do we have?" Lauren asked.

Lauren, with her red hair, made an unlikely vampire, but she did make a pretty one. At thirty, Lauren had added a few more curves to her high school figure, as people who worked at a desk were apt to do.

"I don't know," Charlotte answered. "Two weeks till Halloween. Two more parties?" Charlotte, "Charlie", was also thirty. Short, dark hair, striped shirt, whistle, she looked like the referee she pretended to be. That she taught physical education at a local school enhanced her Halloween image.

"At least two," Monica said. She was the third member of this threesome that had been together almost since nappies. She was also the prettiest. Long blonde hair, blue eyes, a figure that looked absolutely wonderful in her short, black mini dress and apron with white lace trim, her thigh high stockings, and saucy headpiece, she was every man's fantasy of a naughty French maid. "Maybe three," she added.

"Three? I think I'm going to puke." Lauren weaved to one side.

"Don't fight it," Charlie said. "Better to get it out than to let it bubble up your throat."

113

"Oh, great," Lauren said. "That's wonderful advice."

A cloud crossed the moon, and the street turned noticeably darker. Monica blinked, checking to see if it was her eyes.

To one side, Charlie grabbed Lauren's arm, steading her. They were coming home late because it had been a good costume party.

Plenty of alcohol and snacks and people who thought they were clever, and some of them were. Monica had been particularly captivated by a superhero in tights who had painted a big 'S' on his bare chest. At some point during the party, she discovered that the 'S' was edible—at least a woman in a nurse costume thought so. Well, maybe the nurse just wanted to lick Superman's skin. That seemed OK too.

"Is it getting colder, or is it me?' Monica asked.

"If you wore a skirt that covered your arse, you might be a bit warmer," Charlie said.

"French Maids don't wear long skirts," Monica answered.

"I need to get home," Lauren said. "I'm going to be sick."

"We're on our way," Charlie said. "We're on our way."

Ahead, a single, faint streetlight cast a small circle of light. Despite being intoxicated, Monica could see why the streets were dangerous at night. There was no way to know if something evil lurked in the shadows. A single woman would make a likely victim.

For a moment, she wondered how that thought slipped into her mind.

She was with two friends, and there was no danger within a hundred miles. She shook her head to clear the thought as it started to drizzle.

"Oh, great," Lauren said. "Cold and wet."

"It's just a mist," Charlie said. "We'll be home and warm before you know it."

"Who had the best costume?" Monica asked, trying to change the subject.

"That's easy," Charlie said. "The princess."

"The princess?" Lauren said. "Wasn't she a crossdresser? I thought she was a he."

"Not a chance," Charlie said. "I talked to her. She's definitely female."

"I don't know how you can tell," Monica said. "Anymore, the he's look like she's and the she's look like he's."

"Anyway," Lauren said and burped. "I thought the guy dressed like Dracula looked the best. I thought his fangs were real."

"That's because you're a vampire," Charlie said. "Bats stick together."

Lauren laughed briefly.

"Oh god, don't make me laugh. My head is spinning."

"I thought Superman was right up there," Monica said. "Pecs and abs, ladies, pecs and abs."

"Oh, I'm sick," Lauren said. "Get me home."

The rain fell harder, more than a drizzle but not yet a downpour. Monica knew her pigtails would soon look like drowned rats sticking out from her head.

Her tight blouse would be more fitting for a wet T-shirt contest than a costume party.

If she hadn't been mostly drunk, she would have been upset — that and the fact that she didn't have to work the next day.

"Well," Monica began. "If you want to get home as fast as possible, we can take our old route."

"Through the cemetery?" Lauren asked. "That one?"

"That one," Monica answered.

"It's dark," Charlie said. "We never went that way in the dark."

"It's a cemetery," Monica said. "Dead bodies buried under six feet of dirt. I don't think we have to worry."

"I don't know... Kahil warned me to be careful what I did around Halloween. She said everything ramps up."

"Charlie. COME ON. You don't really believe that!"

"I've got an open mind. Just because you don't believe in ghosts."

"I know about your psychic," Monica said to Charlie, "and I'm guessing she talks to the spirits all the time. But, frankly, I don't buy it. I mean, I've done some research."

"You didn't do any research, your assistant did," Charlie said.

"Well OK, but I read what she found. And trust me, she didn't find any evidence of the afterlife."

"You're like all the others, mind closed to what are infinite possibilities."

"Stop arguing," Lauren said. "Get me home. God, how many streetlights are there?"

"One," Charlie answered. "Why?"

"I hate double vision."

Monica reached out and grabbed Lauren's arm. "Come on, we'll cut through the cemetery, and we'll be home thirty minutes earlier."

"I don't think that's a good idea," Charlie said.

"Nonsense," Monica said. "It's raining and cold, and Lauren is about to pass out.

Want to carry her home? Charlie glanced at Monica but said nothing as Monica turned into an alley.

Lauren leaned heavily on Monica's arm, barely keeping her balance. While the street had been dark, it was like a neon-lit arcade compared to the alley. Monica was half thankful for the cold rain as it probably kept the rats at bay. Not that she was particularly scared of rats—as long as they maintained a proper distance. The alley was theirs. She was willing to grant them ownership. If they didn't run over her toes, she was happy.

"What's that smell?" Lauren asked. "It's making me sick."

"Rubbish," Charlie answered. "Breathe through your mouth."

"We'll be through this soon," Monica added. "Hang on."

They moved quickly through the alley. Her TV station had run a program about muggings, and she knew alleys housed almost as many muggers as rats.

They walked along another street with a distant streetlight, Lauren moaning and Charlie silent.

Monica asked herself why she hadn't left with Superman when he had asked. She would be home by now. But she wouldn't be with her friends. They had developed a kind of pact. No one could leave with someone new. Phone numbers were fine. Arranging a date was fine. But if the women arrived together, they left together. Monica was thankful for that. Just before they left the alley, they stopped as a wet, black cat scampered past.

"Was that a rat?" Lauren asked.

"A cat," Charlie said. "A black cat."

"Come on," Monica said.

"It's bad luck, isn't it?" Lauren asked.

"We're not going to worry about bad luck," Monica said. "The rain is unlucky enough."

The arch over the path announced their destination — STONE STREET CEMETERY.

A yellow light shone on the name, reminding Monica of her school days. The three of them had often giggled their way through this entrance. Sometimes, they ran, and if they did, Charlie always won. More often, they walked, chatting about school and boys and teachers and homework. Rain, sun, fog, they used the path often.

But never at night.

Charlie had been right about that. They had never walked through the rows of headstones and graves in the dark.

Monica wasn't sure if that was because they had been scared or because they hadn't really had the opportunity. In those days, perhaps Charlie had purposely steered them around the cemetery. If she did, Monica never noticed. Avoiding a dark cemetery seemed like a bright idea.

"Why is it so effing dark?" Lauren asked.

"It's night," Charlie answered.

Lauren fumbled through her purse until she found her phone. Blinking, she tapped the screen until the torch app came up. Suddenly, a beam of light shone ahead of her.

"That's better," Lauren said.

"Your battery is going to die in like a minute," Charlie said.

"I don't care," Lauren said. "I hate to walk in the dark." They were halfway through the cemetery when Monica felt the urge. "Oh god," she said suddenly stopping and crossing her legs. "I have to stop."

"What?" Charlie asked. "We can't stop, not here."

Monica danced around in circles. "I can't wait." She stepped off the path into the dark.

"I'm going to puke," Lauren said.

"I can't believe the both of you. You can't be doing this," Charlie said. "This is a graveyard!"

"It's not like I'm not going to wee on a grave," Monica said from out of the dark. She moved around a headstone and onto some grass. The problem was that in the rainy dark, it was impossible to know exactly where she was.

She hoped it wasn't a grave, and she hoped she could hurry up and finish what she was doing before someone else came along. All she needed was some Bobby or caretaker coming by. How long would she have her job if that story got into the tabloids? Not long. She tried to hurry, but she was not a practiced camper.

"Hurry," Lauren said. "My phone is dying."

"Smile," Charlie said.

Monica looked up, and Charlie's phone flashed.

"You took my picture?"

"Hurry up, or I'll sell it to the Guardian."

"You wouldn't dare. Of course I wouldn't Ms Stanford."

"At least, not tonight. I'll save it for when I need a favour."

Monica heard Charlie move off giggling.

"Want to see a picture of our esteemed telly friend?" Charlie said. "That's Monica," Lauren said. "But why is she squatting on someone's grave?"

"Oh god," Charlie said yelled. "Monica, get out of there!"

Monica came sheepishly around the headstone to find Charlie and Lauren looking at Charlie's phone.

"Show me," Monica said.

Charlie showed Monica the photo, and the headstone behind Monica was clearly visible.

"Delete it," Monica said. "Delete it now."

"I will, I will," Charlie said.

"OUCH!" Lauren's voice sounded from the dark.

Charlie and Monica turned to Lauren who had stepped off the path and tripped over a low grave marker. They hurried over and helped Lauren to her feet.

"Let's get out of here," Charlie said. "This is getting eerie."

Charlie took Lauren's left arm, and Monica took Lauren's right. Even though Monica didn't feel scared, she agreed with Charlie. It was time to leave the cemetery. Weird things begat weird things. Or, as they said at the station—bad luck comes in threes.

It was raining harder as they exited the cemetery. Monica was soaked and cold as a brisk wind arose. Why hadn't they called a cab? They would be safe and warm and not worried about bad juju or karma or whatever people called retribution for weeing on a grave. Luckily, Lauren's house was only a block away. Actually, it was her parents' house. Lauren had bought it from them so they could retire to the north. Lauren lived alone which was fine since it was a small house.

"I'm going to be sick," Lauren said as they reached the house.

Lauren closed one eye and tried to smile. "Thanks, mates, I don't think I could have done it without you." Then, she started giggling. "You two look so funny. I want a pic."

Monica and Charlie watched Lauren fumble with her purse... and fumble with her purse.

"It's not here," Lauren said.

"What's not there?" Monica asked.

"My phone. It's not here. I lost it."

"Check your pockets," Charlie said. "You probably misplaced it."

Monica watched as Lauren checked the few pockets in her vampire costume. "It's not here," Lauren said.

"Then, you lost it," Charlie said.

"We have to go find it," Lauren said.

"You're in no condition to look for anything tonight. Tomorrow is soon enough," Monica said.

"You don't understand," Lauren said. "My client list is on that phone. I can't lose it."

"We don't have any idea where you lost it," Charlie said. "And it's raining. Go to bed."

"The cemetery, I lost it in the cemetery. Remember, I was using the torch, and then, and then..."

"We're not going back to the cemetery in the dark," Monica said. "But I promise we'll be back in the morning. Then, we'll all go find your phone. All right?"

Lauren began to cry. "I need my phone."

"Not tonight, Lauren. You're not making any deals tonight."

Charlie gently turned Lauren and helped her up the steps and in through the front door. "Go in and sleep. We'll be back in the morning."

Monica waited on the walk as Charlie coaxed Lauren into the house.

Since she couldn't get any wetter, Monica didn't mind too much. "I'm guessing she won't remember losing her phone," Charlie said as she re-joined Monica.

"She never does," Monica said. "Next time, we dump her in a cab."

"Along with you and me."

They laughed as they trudged through the rain. Luckily. Charlie's flat wasn't far, and the rain didn't get worse. The two-floor climb to the flat tired Monica more than she wanted to admit. She felt the effects of the alcohol.

"When will your new house be ready?" Charlie asked as she tossed a towel to Monica.

"Monday, and I can't thank you enough for the last week." Monica undid her pigtails and vigorously dried her hair.

"You're welcome, and I'm sure you'll find a way of paying me back. Good night."

Monica watched Charlie disappear into the bedroom before she went to the loo and stripped off her wet clothes. She draped them over the tub to dry and slipped into her PJ's. As she brushed her teeth, she wondered if she had really done a wee on someone's grave. That thought made her shudder.

That was really bad luck, wasn't it? Like walking under a ladder or opening an umbrella indoors? Although, she would have paid a pretty penny for an umbrella before she left the party. After making her bed on the sofa, Monica turned out the light and closed her eyes. Then, she opened them as a cloud moved, and the moon shone through the window

For a moment, Monica swore she saw a figure looking into the room, a face but not really a face. She blinked and the face was gone. She shivered as she watched the window for a full minute. The face didn't appear, and she presumed she had imagined the entire episode. That was the last thing she remembered before Charlie shook her awake.

"Come on," Charlie said. "Get dressed. Lauren's not answering her home phone."

Chapter Two - The Consequence

Monica was up and dressed in a flash. While they had walked the night before, this being Sunday, they drove Monica's car to Lauren's house. When they found the front door unlocked, Monica frowned at Charlie.

"Lauren usually locks it, doesn't she?"

Charlie nodded and pushed open the door.

"Should we go in?" Monica asked. "I mean, if something happened, shouldn't we call the police?"

"The door's unlocked. She's our friend. We don't have time for Bobbies."

The house was exactly as Monica remembered, nothing was out of place, but she was still surprised to find the lights on.

"She's probably passed out," Charlie said as she led the way to the bedroom.

But Lauren was not passed out. In fact, she wasn't in the bedroom. More importantly, her bed had not been slept in.

"Check the house," Monica said. "Let's see if we can find her."

It took less than five minutes for Charlie and Monica to look into every room and closet. When they met back by the front door, they frowned at one another.

"She's not here," Charlie said.

"She wasn't here all night. You don't suppose…"

"As drunk as she was, she wasn't going out to meet some chap."

"Where are her clothes?" Monica asked.

"Her what?"

"Her wet clothes. She was as soaked as we were. Her wet vampire costume should be here somewhere."

"I didn't see it."

"Neither did I."

They nodded at the same time.

"Her phone," Charlie said.

"The cemetery," Monica said.

They hurried along the street, not bothering with the car, but cutting across the backstreets and passing through the alley way.

"That dumb skirt," Charlie said as they entered the back gate into the cemetery "In the dark and rain, what could she hope to find?"

"Her client list. Like she couldn't find more clients. I swear, when I find that girl I'm going to give a good chat. She can't be doing things like this."

They hurried along the still wet and slippery path.

"It's just ahead, isn't it?" Charlie asked.

"What's just ahead?" Monica answered.

"Where we stopped, where you had a wee on a grave."

"Don't, Charlie, don't say that out loud. It's bad enough that I did it...without knowing it. I don't need anyone reminding me."

They turned a corner and spotted Lauren. Charlie stopped dead for a split second then sprinted forward. When she reached her, her voice wailed out, "Oh God. No. It can't be" A weight dropped in Monica's stomach.

"I'll call emergency", she called in an unnaturally high-pitched voice. Monica punched the key pad. She didn't have to say much. The dispatcher assured Monica that help was on the way. Had Monica been with Charlie and Lauren, she would have told the dispatcher that the help needn't hurry. As soon as Monica saw Lauren's blue face she knew that the worst had happened.

On one knee, Charlie looked up, tears in her eyes. Monica knelt and wrapped an arm around Charlie. Monica didn't say anything. There was nothing to say. They cried together until the police arrived.

For the police, it was easy. Lauren tripped, hit her head, and became unconscious. Then she aspirated; she choked on her own vomit. Just another young woman who had behaved recklessly and had too much to drink. Case closed. For Monica, it wasn't that simple. It was a guilt trip because she could have stayed the night with Lauren. If Monica had, Lauren would be alive.

Monica told herself over and over that it wasn't her fault. Over and over, she felt a twinge of pain. Even Lauren's parents had told Monica and Charlie through their tears that Lauren's death was not their fault, it was a tragic wasted life brought on by bad judgement. And they should be grateful they were still here, and to live their lives to the fullest making every moment count. As if that erased the guilt. It was after the funeral, while they sipped punch at Lauren's house, that Charlie took Monica aside.

"You think it was an accident?" Charlie asked. Monica rubbed her temples, she didn't feel like listening to Charlies juju superstition.

"Of course, what else could it be?"

"Remember what you did?"

"Yeah, I got drunk. So did you."

"No, on the way home, remember the cemetery?"

"Of course, I remember the cemetery I had to have a wee so what?"

"You did it on a grave. On a person's grave. Have any idea what that might do? Especially at bloody Halloween."

"Nothing, absolutely nothing. Blokes take a leak all over graves and headstones all the time. Do they die?"

"You're not listening. Kahil says that sometimes spirits take offense when someone disrespects their grave. And they get back at them."

"Is this Kahil, the psychic?"

"Kahil is very knowledgeable about spiritual things."

"Kahil is a sinkhole for quid. What do you expect her to say? That spirits love when a chap waters the grave?"

"I'm just saying that if you did something on the wrong grave, the spirit might have taken it out on Lauren."

"Don't be daft. Lauren died because she made an incredibly bad decision, which isn't hard to believe since she was DEAD DRUNK. She paid for her stupidity."

Charlie took a step back. "You didn't like Lauren?"

Monica rubbed her face. "I loved Lauren. We both did. But I'm not about to accept responsibility for her death."

Charlie backed away.

"Wait," Monica said.

"What happens next is on your head," Charlie said.

"Oh, come on Charlie you don't mean that, let's talk."

Charlie shook her head, turned, and walked away. Monica let her go. She knew better than to test Charlie's belief in the supernatural. Charlie had been partial to ghosts and spirits and paranormal phenomena since school.

"You're coming to the house warming," Monica called.

Charlie didn't answer.

The Haunting of Stone Street Cemetery

Available at

http://a-fwd.to/1txL6vk

Other Titles by Cat Knight

The Haunting of Elleric Lodge

Available here: http://a-fwd.to/6aa9uON

The Haunting of Fairview House

Available here: http://a-fwd.to/6lKwbG1

The Haunting of Weaver House

Available here: http://a-fwd.to/7Do5KDi

The Haunting of Grayson House

Available here: http://a-fwd.to/3nu8fqk

The Haunting of Keira O'Connell

Available here: http://a-fwd.to/2qrTERv

The Haunting of Ferncoombe Manor

Available here: http://a-fwd.to/32MzXfz

The Haunting of Highcliff Hall

Available here: http://a-fwd.to/2Fsd7F6

About the Author

Cat Knight has been fascinated by fantasy and the paranormal since she was a child. Where others saw animals in clouds, Cat saw giants and spirits. A mossy rock was home to faeries, and laying beneath the earth another dimension existed. That was during the day. By night there were evil spirits lurking in the closet and under her bed. They whirled around her in the witching hour, daring her to come out from under her blanket and face them. She breathed in a whisper and never poked her head out from under her covers nor got up in the dark no matter how scared she was, because for sure, she would die at the hands of ghosts or demons. How she ever grew up without suffocating remains a mystery.

RECEIVE THE HAUNTING OF LILAC HOUSE FREE!

http://eepurl.com/c4zKTb

Never Miss A book

Subscribe to Cat Knight's newsletter for new release announcements

http://eepurl.com/cKReuz

Like me on Facebook

https://www.facebook.com/catknightauthor/

Printed in Great Britain
by Amazon